THE MATH INSPECTORS

MYSTERY, ADVENTURE, HUMOR... and MATH!

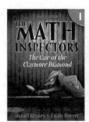  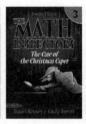 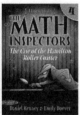

Praise for the Math Inspectors:

"Clever, humorous, and well-written detective mystery series for elementary and middle school readers. The plot kept me guessing and entertained." - B.M.

"This is a fun math series for the eight to tween set with well developed characters who could jump onto the Saturday morning TV screen and find a comfortable home on PBS." - C.Q.

"I bought this for my 10 year-old son who is a voracious reader and loves mysteries, and he just loves the series. It makes math a fun challenge, not a chore, and still managed to entertain my bright child!" -R.B.

WANT TWO FREE STORIES?

SIGN UP FOR MY NO-SPAM NEWSLETTER
AND GET TWO DANIEL KENNEY STORIES,
PLUS ALWAYS BE THE FIRST TO KNOW
ABOUT NEW CONTENT.

ALL FOR FREE.

DETAILS CAN BE FOUND
AT THE END OF THIS BOOK.

THE MATH INSPECTORS

BOOK TWO

The Case of the Mysterious Mr. Jekyll

Daniel Kenney & Emily Boever

TRENDWOODPRESS

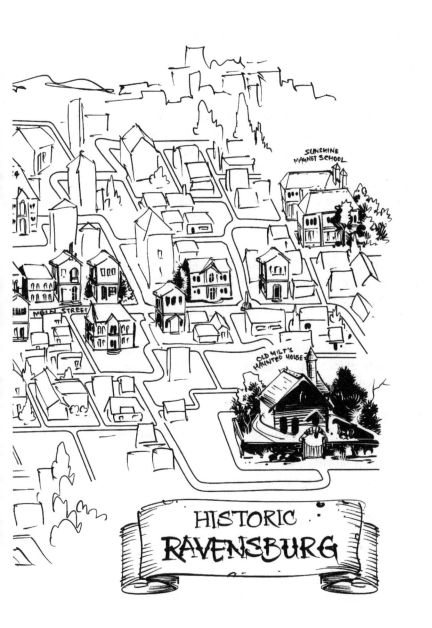

Editing by David Gatewood, www.lonetrout.com
Interior Layout by Polgarus Studios, www.polgarusstudio.com
Cover Design by www.AuthorSupport.com
Illustrations by Sumit Roy, www.scorpydesign.com

Dedication:

To my Grandma and Grandpa McGill.
Daniel Kenney

To my parents, Jerry and Drew Black. I love you.
Emily Boever.

Table of Contents

Gertie ♡ FELIX STANLEY Charlotte

CHAPTER ONE

OCTOBER 30, 10:16 P.M.

A full moon rose over the town of Ravensburg, bathing it in a cold, blue light. A masked figure stole along the streets, melting into the long shadows. On the corner of Oak and Vanderbilt, the figure paused under a row of tall bushes and looked up at the sky.

The final approach was always the most difficult part of any job. Patience was key.

When clouds covered the moon, the figure left the cover of the bushes and raced across Ida Rainey's lawn and up to her back door, where the motion-sensing light had been disarmed the night before.

The figure removed a bone from a large green satchel and slipped it through the swinging doggy door. Little feet scampered toward the door, and one bark escaped the animal before it attacked the bone with squeaks of delight.

Ten seconds later, right on time, a thud sounded. The dog had hit the floor.

The figure smiled, pulled the sleeping dog through the doggy door, opened the satchel again, and went to work.

An electric razor buzzed to life. Then the click-clack of an aerosol can, followed by several long hissing noises.

When the masterpiece was complete, the sleeping dog was slid carefully back inside through the door, and the bone was collected.

The masked figure grabbed the satchel and melted back into the shadows.

CHAPTER TWO

HALLOWEEN

"My grandpa claims Old Milt's is the best haunted house in the world," said Gertie. "And I said, 'The *world*, Grandpa? I mean, what about Transylvania, for starters? The home of Dracula has to have some pretty killer haunted houses.'"

Holding Stanley's hand, she followed Charlotte, Felix, and Stanley down the dark, creaky, third-floor hallway of Old Milt's—Ravensburg's most popular Halloween hangout.

"Look, guys." Charlotte pointed at several dark blobs the size of horses dangling from the ceiling. "Spiders. How cute."

Felix looked up. "I was partial to the giant leeches last year. But that's just me. How 'bout you, Stanley?"

Stanley looked up at the giant spiders. They

reminded him of that one he'd seen in *The Lord of the Rings.* He shivered.

"Stanley," Gertie hissed, "you're cutting off the circulation in my wrist."

"Oh, sorry," Stanley whispered. He could hear his voice shake as the words came out.

"I still can't believe he came," said Charlotte.

Felix laughed. "What, you mean because Stanley always promises he'll come here with us on Halloween, but *every* year for the last three years he's only made it as far as the parking lot?"

"Don't listen to them, Stanley," Gertie said. "You're doing great. You only squealed like a little baby five or six times, by my count. And you haven't cried once."

Gertie held open a hole in the spider web. Stanley shut his eyes and stepped through. She patted him on the arm. "See, I told you nothing was going to happen. We're almost done. I think there's only one more big—"

"RAAAAAAHHHHHHHH!"

A slimy hand shot out of nowhere, grabbed Stanley, and pulled him toward a gaping black hole in the wall.

Stanley screamed bloody murder.

Gertie immediately fell to the ground, grabbed Stanley's legs, and employed a deadweight technique to win the tug-of-war. It wasn't working.

Stanley's eyes were wide open now, and lights flashed from every direction, each one revealing a new terror. He couldn't see what had hold of him, but it was dragging him straight for that hole in the wall—which Stanley now realized was an enormous open mouth. He was only steps away.

"Gertie, help! I'm too young to die!" he cried.

Gertie was still wrapped around his ankles, like an anchor skipping along the ocean floor. With each stride toward the hole she squealed, "Best... haunted house... ever!"

"Felix! Charlotte! Get me out of here!" Stanley screamed.

Felix exchanged a grin with Charlotte. "He might actually enjoy the ride."

"I doubt it," Charlotte said. "But it'll be good for him. Gertie, let go."

"Let go?" Stanley shouted. "You can't—"

He felt Gertie's arms release his ankles, and he was jerked backward into the gaping jaws of his own worst nightmare. Gertie's voice echoed off the walls behind him: "Embrace it, Stanley! Embrace it!"

Stanley flopped onto his back and tumbled headlong down a dark twisting tunnel. Hands grabbed at him. Spider webs stuck to him. Glowing eyes stared right through him.

Stanley screamed louder than he'd ever screamed in his whole life.

And just when he thought he couldn't go any faster, Stanley shot out of the tunnel, through the cool night air, and into a pit of something spongy.

He was alive.

He breathed a sigh of relief.

And then he opened his eyes.

He'd landed in an enormous pit of monkey heads.

He screamed again.

"Sweet tumble, dude."

Stanley looked up. A teenager with a nametag that read "Ricky" was holding out a hand to help him up.

"Anybody who rides the Tunnel of Death gets a stuffed monkey head," Ricky said. "Do you prefer Boogers or Vomit?"

Stanley unfolded from the fetal position. "Excuse

me?" he said. He felt another rush of panic as he climbed out of the pit.

Ricky pulled out two monkey heads. He shook the yellow one first. "This guy's named Boogers." Then he shook the green one. "And this cute little fella is Vomit. Which one do you want?"

"Neither," Stanley mumbled.

Ricky shrugged. "Most kids pick Boogers." He stuck the yellow one in Stanley's arms and walked away.

As Stanley stumbled over to a bench, he made a mental note to avoid Old Milt's, the Tunnel of Death, and Ricky for the rest of his life. Why Gertie and the rest of these people thought it was so fun to be scared, he would never know. To Stanley Carusoe, there was almost nothing worse in the world. He took off his glasses, put his head between his knees, and tried to calm himself.

"Hey, loser!" barked a gruff voice.

Stanley recognized that gruff voice. It belonged to none other than Dervin Chowder, the school bully. Stanley jumped, expecting the voice to be talking to him. Instead, the insult was being hurled at Herman Dale.

Herman was small, dressed funny, and didn't talk very much. But mostly, Herman was the new kid. And while Dervin was usually an equal opportunity bully, Stanley noticed that these days he seemed to have a special place in his small brain set aside for Herman.

Herman turned away from Dervin and walked away from Old Milt's alone. Dervin and his pals laughed as they headed inside the haunted house.

Stanley considered going after Herman, but just then another voice called out, and Stanley jumped again.

"Yo, Stanley, that was awesome!"

Felix, Charlotte, and Gertie came running out of Old Milt's.

"The Tunnel of Death, Stanley!" Gertie said. "I've *never* gotten to ride down the Tunnel of Death! You're so lucky."

"Yeah, real lucky," Stanley said. "I want to thank each of you, my *former* best friends in the whole world, for helping me out in my time of need." He handed Gertie the yellow monkey head.

"Aw, Boogers!" she squeaked. "Seriously, guys, how cute is this little guy? So, Stanley, for real: how was the slide?"

Stanley shook his head. "I—I don't want to talk about it."

"The man's right." Felix thumped him on the back. "At a time like this, we should all be talking less and eating more. Who's up for an *Under Doggie*?"

"I don't know," said Charlotte, looking at Stanley

out of the corner of her eye. "Maybe we should head home."

Gertie nodded. "Yeah, Under Doggies always sounds like a good idea, but they never end up that way."

"Come on, guys," Felix said. "It's a Halloween tradition. Besides, the line's already a mile long. And maybe he's changed."

"There are only a few things in life that will never change, Felix," said Stanley. "Most of them are math formulas. Another one is Frank Under."

But despite Stanley's reservations, the friends followed Felix to the end of an amazingly straight line leading to the walk-up window of a run-down food shack. They put their arms straight at their sides and prepared to move in unison, left foot first.

"I'm definitely adding chocolate to my Triple Chili Chihuahua this year," Felix whispered over his shoulder.

"Shut it, Felix," Gertie snapped. "What are you trying to do?"

The ramshackle hot dog stand reminded Stanley of Old Milt's. An ancient rusty sign with big blue letters spelled out "Under Doggies." Smaller letters underneath read "Frank Under: Hotdog Genius." Stanley imagined his parents standing in this line when they were kids. He wondered how *they* had dealt with Mr. Under.

As the first girl in line came away with her order, she was sobbing loudly. The boy who came away from the stand next was sobbing, too. But the next three kids only had tears in their eyes. Then the boy right in front of Felix walked away without even ordering. He looked like he was going to be sick.

Finally it was Felix's turn.

"Next!" barked Mr. Under from inside the shack. "What do you want, you big red beanpole?"

Felix stepped up, left leg first, put exact change on the counter, and said loudly, "May I please have one extra-large Triple Chili Chihuahua, smothered in chocolate and horseradish, please?"

"The Belcher Special, eh?" said Mr. Under, wiping greasy hands on the dirty dishtowel slung over his left shoulder. "Well, I suppose since you don't have any friends, it doesn't matter what comes out of your mouth once you put something into it. Does it?"

Felix didn't move. He didn't even breathe. He just waited.

After a minute, Mr. Under slid Felix his order. "Happy Halloween, beanpole. Now get out of my sight before I puke."

Felix grabbed his Chihuahua and turned away at a precise forty-five degree angle.

"Next!" growled Mr. Under.

Gertie stepped forward. "May I please have one small—"

"I said NEXT!" screamed Mr. Under.

He stuck his head out of the window and looked up, down, left and right, like he was trying to find something. His few remaining strands of gray hair flopped with every movement. "I don't see anybody here," he said. "Where could she be?" Then he looked down at Gertie and grabbed at his heart. "Oh, there you are. Don't sneak up on me like that. What do you want?"

Gertie's ears turned red. She answered in short bursts of controlled anger. "May I please have one small litter of Wiener Pups, please?"

Mr. Under looked at her for a moment. Then he put a hand to the side of his mouth, like he was being confidential, and said, "Are you sure that's good for your diet?"

Stanley had never seen Gertie show this much self-restraint in her life. Her ears turned a brighter red, but she didn't say anything.

Mr. Under laughed heartily, threw a brown bag at her, and jerked his head to the side. "Off you go,

Pudgy. Happy eating."

Gertie turned away at a precise forty-five-degree angle. Her chest was puffed out, her head held high, and, Stanley noticed, her eyes were full of rage.

Charlotte stepped up to the counter next. She looked straight into Mr. Under's eyes and didn't say a word. He held her gaze for an instant, then grabbed the order that had been pushed to the counter by his cook and handed it to her. "A medium order of Manicured Poodle Puffs, as usual."

Charlotte paid, got her change, and moved aside for Stanley.

Stanley approached the counter nervously. "May I please have a medium order of Old Yeller Bites, please?" he said.

Mr. Under sneered, wiped snot from his nose, then took Stanley's money. He pushed a bag stuffed with fluffy yellow squares across the counter. Stanley grabbed the bag, but Under held it tight and looked Stanley right in the eyes.

Stanley was too afraid to blink. He started to loosen his hold on the bag.

"Just what I thought," said Under. "You're a

coward. How about I throw in a large order of Fraidy Cats with that?" He laughed and let go of the bag.

Stanley took his order and wobbled away to the condiment station around the corner of the shack. He pumped ketchup into a white container under a sign that read: "You Know You'll Be Back."

He found the others seated at a picnic table.

Gertie was just staring at her food. "How do you get away with not being picked on every year, Charlotte?"

Charlotte tossed a Poodle Puff in the air and caught it in her mouth. "He's like any other bully. You show them once that they can't hurt you, and they'll leave you alone."

"Easier said than done," Gertie muttered. "Here, Felix, I'm not hungry anymore."

Felix smiled as he accepted her Wiener Pups. "I'll tell you what *I* do," he said. "I just turn my brain off entirely when it's my turn. Don't even hear a thing. Not that I'd mind anything Mr. Under wanted to say, as long as he keeps cooking up greatness."

Stanley sighed. "Well, you're right about one

thing. This is the greatest food I've ever eaten."

After they'd finished eating—and Felix had finished belching the alphabet—they turned toward home. But when they came to the corner where they usually parted ways, Stanley hesitated. Those last few blocks to his house looked a little spookier than usual, and he was glad the conversation hadn't yet died down.

"Well, I'm off to get free candy," said Felix. He undid the buttons on his shirt and pulled it open to reveal another shirt underneath. A shirt with a giant S on it. "What a holiday!"

"Oh," Charlotte teased, "so there's actually a point in you wearing that, um, spandexy thing?"

Felix pulled off his shirt and pants, unfurled his cape, put his hands on his hips, and thrust out his chest. "I'll have you know that this is an officially licensed Superman costume. Do you have any idea what it cost me?"

"Besides your pride, you mean?" Charlotte asked. "When will these boys ever grow up, Gertie?"

"You're asking the wrong person, Charlotte." Gertie took a pair of thick-rimmed glasses out of her purse and pulled her hair into a tight bun. She looked at Felix. "Ready, Clark?"

"After you, Lois."

And they were off in a single bound.

Charlotte looked over at Stanley, who was still staring blankly down his darkened street. "You all right, Stanley?" she asked.

Stanley tried not to sound scared. "Me? Oh, yeah, sure, no problem. Couldn't be better. Happy Halloween!" He took off down the sidewalk, trying to look calm and collected.

But as soon as Charlotte was out of sight, he bolted for home. And in an effort to get home as quickly as possible, he even risked the shortcut through Mrs. Dinklage's overgrown bushes.

That was a mistake.

As he pushed his way through the tangled shrubbery, something grabbed his foot. He looked down—and there, looking back up at him and moaning loudly, was a ghost.

Stanley screamed.

He jerked his foot loose and continued to push through the bushes, only to run into an enormous spider web. Frantically wiping at his face, he cleared his vision, only to find he was looking into two enormous red eyes.

Stanley's breath was gone, his body shaking hard. He turned away from the eyes, and in one final effort, he cleared the bushes and ran for his house.

But standing between him and the Carusoe home was a dark figure with a white face and two colorless oval holes for eyes. The figure held a broad silver sword above its head and shouted, "Thou know'st 'tis common; all that lives must die, passing through nature to eternity."

Stanley screamed at the top of his lungs and collapsed to the ground.

CHAPTER THREE

AT WAR!

Flashlights turned on all around him, and the moaning turned to laughter.

The red-eyed figure removed his mask. Darren Simpson.

The white ghost stepped forward. Lena Mills.

Another figure appeared, holding a giant spider web. Ronan White.

Stanley let out a long growl. Of course. The English Club.

"Hey, Stanley," said the masked figure with the sword—Polly Partridge. "You like math so well, so tell me: what's the probability you just peed your pants?"

The four English snobs roared in laughter.

Stanley stood and brushed himself off. He was

trying to regain his breath, and his body still shook uncontrollably. "I bet anybody would be scared if you snuck up on them in the middle of the night," he said. "Not a big accomplishment, Polly. But of course, you *are* the English Club. You're not used to big accomplishments."

Polly tore off her mask and stepped forward. Even by the glow of a flashlight, and wearing a pound of scary makeup, her long brown hair and fine features were impressive. Why someone this pretty had to be so miserable, Stanley had no idea.

Polly and her posse closed the circle around him.

"What are you going to do?" said Stanley. "Outline me to death?"

"Listen, Stanley, having Chief Abrams call me out on television was below the belt," Polly said.

"So this little ambush is your way of getting even?"

"Not a chance. This is simply a warning, prompted by the universal rules of fair play. Consider yourself at war, Stanley Carusoe. You and the rest of the Math Nerdigans."

"Speaking of war, Polly, do you know when the

War of 1812 was? Oh, wait... probably not, since it involves a number. Now, why don't you and your poetry-loving chums go read Bob Shakespeare and light some candles in a cave somewhere?"

"It's William Shakespeare, you beef-witted jolt-head."

"Yeah, well, I hear he's good, too."

Polly stepped right up to him. "Like I said, Stanley: *At. War.*"

She poked a finger into his chest and glared at him. He didn't blink.

Finally, she snapped her fingers. "Come on, guys. Let's get out of here before the coffee shop closes."

Stanley watched them leave. Then he sprinted the last twenty feet to his house, jumped up the steps to his porch, and slipped inside as quickly as he could.

CHAPTER FOUR

TOP SECRET

"What a bunch of creeps," Charlotte said. She barely missed banking the six ball into the side slot. She looked up at Stanley. "I knew I should have walked you home last night. What did they do after that?"

"They just ran off to the coffee shop," Stanley said.

They were in Charlotte's basement, taking advantage of the day-after-Halloween late start to squeeze in a game of eight ball. That 1970s fake wood paneling ran along the walls, and thick brown carpet covered the floor. The basement was just wide enough to hold a pool table, and the four friends made it a ritual to come here every time school started late.

Felix sighed. "That's not right, buddy. That's not

right at all. And you're sure Polly was involved?"

Gertie rolled her eyes. "For the last time, Felix Dervish, Polly Partridge doesn't even know you're alive. And even if she did, she's the enemy. Now get it right!"

Felix gulped. "A very *cute* enemy."

"Felix!" Gertie growled.

"Okay, okay, I get it. Polly's the enemy. A foul, vile, nefarious villain. Blah, blah, blah, blah, blah."

Gertie turned to Stanley. "So, do you finally understand what a menace she is?"

Stanley lined up a difficult shot. "I've always understood that," he said, "but Polly's never declared war on us before. We've got to be prepared. One ball—corner pocket."

The cue ball struck its target squarely and spun backward to set up the next shot. The solid yellow ball hit the side wall, then bounced off sharply and disappeared into the corner pocket.

"You have any ideas?" Charlotte asked.

"We should definitely spy on her," Felix said. "Them—I mean, we should spy on *them*."

"Doesn't even know you're alive," Gertie said

again as she chalked her pool stick.

Stanley's cell phone rang. He glanced at the number and looked up in surprise. "It's Evans." He answered. "Hi, Officer Evans, what's up?" Stanley listened and nodded. Finally he gave his friends a thumbs-up. "If you think we can help. Yeah, we've got time right now. Thanks!"

Stanley snapped his phone shut. "War will have to wait. Duty calls."

"It's about time," said Gertie.

"To the bat-cycles!" Felix yelled.

*

When the Math Inspectors arrived at Ravensburg Police Station, Officer Evans escorted them into a room with a long wooden table, where they all sat down. Four blue folders lay on the tabletop.

"I made copies of the case file for you guys."

Stanley looked up. "Wait a second. With the Franklin case, you wouldn't let us even see the police report, and now you're giving us the whole file?"

Charlotte nodded. "That's right, Officer Evans,

Stanley asked you for that report. And your exact words were, 'No can do, Stanley. That file is official police business. Like I said, you kids run along home.'"

Gertie drummed her fingers on the table. "So what's changed? It's been six whole weeks since we helped you out with the Claymore Diamond mishap—when we were shamefully treated by this department, by the way. Why is it that you're just now calling us in to help on another case?"

"Yeah," Felix said. "I mean, don't get me wrong. At first, listening to a police scanner for hours on end was a great excuse for extended snacking. But it turns out that things like a robbery-in-progress only happen... well, like, once in this town. We're getting pretty bored."

Evans opened up the file. "You kids done complaining yet?"

Felix put his finger to his chin. "Actually, no, I was wondering where the donuts are."

"Excuse me?" Evans said.

"The donuts. It's a known fact that cops singlehandedly keep the donut industry in business.

I want to know where you keep them all. Secret donut room, right?"

Evans shook his head. "I'm just going to pretend you didn't say that." He held up a sheet from the file. "Guys, we've got a serial criminal on the loose."

"A cereal criminal?" Felix said. "Lucky Charms or Frosted Flakes?"

Charlotte punched him in the shoulder.

"And this *serial* criminal," Evans continued, "calls himself Mr. Jekyll."

"What kind of crimes?" Stanley asked.

"Vandalism. The criminal always writes 'Mr. Jekyll' in blue permanent marker or paint somewhere at the crime scene. We've made very little progress in our investigation, and after discussing it, Chief Abrams and I agreed that a kid's perspective might be helpful."

"Why's that?" Stanley asked.

Evans stood up. "Just take the files and study them. You'll see what I mean. Then, when you're ready, come by the station and give me your thoughts. Okay?"

Stanley picked up the folder in front of him. "So these are ours to keep?"

Evans nodded. "All yours. But don't go showing them around school. Consider this Top Secret. As a matter of fact, it's really important that you don't tell anybody besides your parents that you're helping out on this case—or that this case even exists. So far, we've managed to keep the victims from going public about the crimes. We're hoping that if the criminal doesn't know we're investigating, he'll stick his neck out too far one of these times. Understood?"

The kids nodded.

As soon as Evans left the room, Felix pounded his fist on the table in excitement. "A top secret case. I almost feel like a real police officer. If only I could find those donuts."

As if on cue, the door flew open and Evans threw something to Felix. A chocolate donut with sprinkles. Felix snatched it out of the air with his long arms.

Evans smiled and let the door shut behind him.

Felix took an enormous bite and licked his lips. "Like I said, secret donut room."

CHAPTER FIVE

GREAT DAY FOR FOOTBALL

Stanley slipped into his seat as the school's morning announcements began.

"Goooood morning, Ravensburg Middle School!" Principal Cooling's voice boomed through the intercom. "Hope you all ate lots of candy last night and drove your parents nuts. You'll be happy to hear that our volleyball team won again. That puts us right in the thick of things with playoffs coming up."

Stanley wasn't listening. He was jotting down thoughts about the Mr. Jekyll case.

"Now, for today's meetings," Dr. Cooling went on. "We have the Science Club at 3:07 sharp."

"Boom goes the nitroglycerine!" Blaise Brown and Harry Mendel bumped fists on Stanley's right.

"And the Chess Club at 3:10," Cooling continued.

"Today, we're going to try and keep our emotions in check... mate," chuckled Sheba Tooney on Stanley's left.

"And last but not least," the speaker blared, "mark your calendars for this Friday night, and come out to show your Caterpillar pride as the football team plays the annual rivalry game against our cross-park rivals, the Sunshine Magnet School Fighting Butterflies. This year, Coach Bellum tells me we're going to take back the coveted Crystal Chrysalis."

At the back of the class, Dervin Chowder smashed his fist onto his desk. "We're going to squash those bugs!"

Cooling ended his announcements with his patented saying: "RMS teachers, the class is yours."

Stanley stuffed the case folder into his backpack and pulled out his enormous Social Studies textbook.

"No more Sherlock for now?" Polly's voice hissed from over his shoulder. Her desk was behind his and to the left. She'd been spying on him.

Stanley turned and shot her an icy look. "We've

been hired by your mother to find your humanity. I told her it was an impossible case."

"Mr. Carusoe," barked Coach Bellum at the front of the room, "since you appear to have excess energy today, perhaps you want to go first."

Oh no, Stanley thought. *Please don't make me do this.*

Coach Bellum folded his hands and smiled. "Get on up here, Carusoe. Let's see what you're made of."

Stanley stood, walked to the smart board, and turned around. The class looked at him like a pack of wild dogs ready for their next meal.

"Mr. Carusoe," Coach Bellum said in his fiery pregame speech voice. "What day is today?"

"It's Tuesday, November first, Coach."

Bellum grinned from ear to ear. "And what's that mean, Stanley? Remember, if you don't do it right the first time, we've got all class to figure it out."

Stanley caught sight of Polly. She was leaning forward, a wide smile across her face.

Stanley balled up his fists, swallowed his dignity, and yelled, "That means it's a GREAT DAY FOR FOOTBALL, COACH!"

Stanley felt his cheeks redden as he returned to his seat. Other than Dervin throwing two pencils at Stanley's head, the rest of the class, and the rest of the day, proved to be uneventful.

When Stanley got to his locker at the end of the day, Blaise Brown, who had the locker right next to his, was talking excitedly with Harry Mendel. But as soon as Stanley walked up, they both stopped talking and exchanged a funny look.

"Yes, Harry," Blaise said. "We definitely should go see that movie sometime."

"Movie?" replied Harry. "Ohhh, right." He winked at Blaise. "The *movie*."

Blaise turned toward Stanley and acted startled to see him. "Oh, hi, Stanley," he said. "We didn't notice you were standing right there. Well, we'd better be off to Science Club. It's 3:04 already. Come on, Harry."

Stanley watched them go. The Science Club guys weren't always the smoothest characters in the world. But still...

As he pulled on his jacket, he wondered what they could be up to.

CHAPTER SIX

THAT DARN CAT

Back at Felix's treehouse, the Math Inspectors started going through Mr. Jekyll's crimes.

Gertie pulled out one of the police reports. "Henry Hood, a local mechanic, walked into his shop to find a surprise on all seven cars he was working on. In blue spray paint across the windshields were the words 'Mr. Jekyll.' And what's more, all of the cars' wiper fluid had been replaced with blue ink."

Felix pulled out another. "Maria Lowenstein, cheerleading coach at Ravensburg High. Goes home to choreograph a new cheer in the living room. Finds out too late that her pompoms have been drenched in blue paint. Had to replace her expensive suede couch and entertainment system.

On the handles of her pompoms were the words 'Mr. Jekyll.'"

"The water tower north of town," said Charlotte, smacking pink bubblegum. "Someone painted a face with a frown on one side, and on the other, in great big blue marker, they wrote 'Mr. Jekyll.'"

"And that brings us to Mr. Booboo," said Stanley.

"Wait, there's actually a person named Mr. Booboo?" Felix said.

"No, it's a dog. Mr. Booboo is the Lhasa apso owned by Ida Rainey. Ms. Rainey was awakened by Mr. Booboo's yipping on Halloween morning."

"All small dogs yip," said Gertie.

"Yes, but half of Mr. Booboo's fur had been shaved. And on the area that was shaved, written in blue paint... you guessed it. 'Mr. Jekyll.'"

Felix looked through the folder. "There's got to be ten more of these. All pretty much along the same lines, all with the same calling card: 'Mr. Jekyll' written in blue ink." He looked up. "Why don't *we* have calling cards? Or a donut room, for that matter?"

Charlotte pulled out another police report.

"These crimes are so random. I bet it's some sicko who likes to cause havoc and probably tries to be as random as possible so nobody gets any leads."

Gertie shook her head. "These crimes aren't just random. Every one of them is also very... *funny*. To a kid, I mean. Our parents would be horrified." Gertie held up a picture of a crime scene with a dozen brown mice scampering about. Each sported a pink tutu bearing the tiny blue signature of Mr. Jekyll.

Stanley adjusted his glasses. "So *that's* why Evans wants our perspective. The cops have worked up a profile for Mr. Jekyll—and they're looking for a kid."

"And he thinks the best way to catch a kid is to *use* kids?" Charlotte asked.

Stanley shrugged. "I guess. But I'm not approaching this like a kid. We've got our own methods, so I say we approach this like—"

"THE MATH INSPECTORS!" Felix yelled, jumping straight into the air and kicking his arms and legs out in a scissors move. As he came down, his leg caught the table, causing him to do a backward somersault and land flat on his face.

"Ouch," he whimpered as he peeled his cheek off the wooden planks of the treehouse floor.

Stanley bent down to help him up. "What exactly were you trying to do?"

Felix cringed as if he was still in pain. "Wasn't it obvious? I just figured, as detectives, we're one step away from being superheroes, so whenever we get called into action we should have a thing we'd do. Like yell 'The Math Inspectors!' and make math signs in the air. I'm the multiplication sign. Couldn't you tell?"

Stanley patted him on the shoulder. "You are a very strange human being, Felix. You know that, right?"

"Yeah, I appreciate you noticing. So how we gonna solve this case?"

Stanley spread out all of the crime scene photos. "For starters, we need to make sense of all these crimes."

"So we investigate the crime scenes and victims?" Charlotte asked.

"No," said Stanley. "We'll leave the cops to do that. We're going to start with the math. Maybe if we dig deeper, we'll find a pattern. Felix, think you could find a map of Ravensburg in your house?"

Felix looked offended. "Stanley, my dad has maps of everything known to man."

"Thumbtacks?"

Felix rubbed his chin. "Okay, you got me. I don't think he has a map of thumbtacks."

Stanley closed his eyes and shook his head. "No, Felix. Do you have any thumbtacks?"

Felix's face brightened. "Oh, sure."

"Whiteboard markers?"

"You bet."

"Bernie's Pizza?"

"No, I just finished the last two—"

"Then we need more pizza. We have work to do, and an extra-large pepperoni would hit the spot."

An hour later, the four friends had eaten the pizza and used thumbtacks to mark all the locations on the map where crimes had occurred. Whenever anybody came up with a number or piece of information, Gertie took notes, Felix ran internet searches, Charlotte ran memory searches, and Stanley tried to fit it all together, hoping to come up with something concrete to put on their crime board.

Felix ran a hand through his red curls, forgetting that pizza grease and hair don't play nicely together. "I'm still not seeing a pattern."

"Yeah," said Charlotte. "Still looks random to me."

"Hopeless," said Gertie, passing Felix a napkin. "I say we use the kid-as-criminal angle to our advantage, plant some evidence against Polly and the English Club creeps, and call it a wrap."

Stanley smiled. "Tempting. Or, we could measure the distance between each point on the map and look for the real criminal. Maybe there's a relationship that might give away something about our Mr. Jekyll."

"But there's 14 points," said Felix. "That's a lot of measurements."

"How many measurements?" said Gertie.

"Well, think about it," said Felix. "Say you've got 14 points. If you choose a point, and draw lines connecting that point to each of the other 13 points, you'll have drawn 13 lines. Then choose a second point, and draw lines from *that* point to all the other 13 points, and you'll have drawn 13 more lines. Do the same thing for each point, and you'll have drawn 13 lines, 14 different times."

"What's 14 times 13 again?" Stanley asked.

"182!" shouted Charlotte before Felix was able to get the words out.

Felix growled at her. "Curse you and your photographic memory."

"182?" said Gertie. "That *is* a lot of measurements."

"Well, it's less than that," said Felix. "The thing is, when you draw the lines the way I just described, you'll end up drawing each line twice. See, you'll choose that first point, and you'll draw lines from that point to the other 13 points. But later, when you choose each of those other points, and draw your 13 lines from *them*, that means you'll be drawing one of those lines *back* to that first point. In other words, you'll draw a line from point A to point B, and later, you'll draw a line from point B to point A. You draw each line twice."

"And if drawing each line twice gets you 182 lines..." Stanley said.

"Then drawing each line once gets you half that, or 91," Felix finished. "There are 91 unique measurements between 14 points."

Gertie threw both hands in the air. "Only 91? Well, what are you complaining about, you big lug? Get to work." She punched him in the shoulder for good measure.

Felix set to work measuring the distances between each pair of points. At first he worked alone, but he grumbled so much about whether or not he had enough food in his system to survive what he began calling the "Old 91 Line Calamity" that the others, tired of his whining, finally chipped in to help. It still took a long time, but Stanley insisted they be thorough.

When they were done, they each sat down with a pad of paper and started playing around with the numbers. But an hour after that, they hadn't come up with anything significant.

Charlotte pulled on a light jacket. "I need to go. Dad and I are planning our hunting trip tonight."

Gertie yawned. "I should head out, too. I've looked at that map so long, my eyes keep crossing."

"Yeah, me too," said Felix. "I've got a little light reading to do before bed." He pulled a book out of his bag: *A Dummy's Guide to Outsmarting Cats.* "How about you, Stanley?"

Stanley looked up blankly. "I'll stay here a little longer. I hate ending the first night on the job without a single lead, and, well, I don't even have any funny feelings."

Charlotte had just started to open the trap door when she suddenly froze. She put a finger to her lips and cocked her head slightly toward the open window on the back of the treehouse. And then they all heard it—a creaking of boards on the balcony.

"There's somebody out there," she whispered.

"What do we do?" Felix whispered back.

"Let's flush them out," Charlotte said. "Gertie, you secure the front window. Felix and I will move to the back window. Stanley, as soon as we're in position, you go through the trap door and climb the rope to the balcony. Hopefully you'll startle them and send them running through the window to escape—and then Felix and I will nab them."

Everyone moved into position. Everyone except

Stanley, who remained seated at the table. Charlotte widened her eyes at him and pointed at the trap door. *Go*, she mouthed.

But Stanley still didn't move. He wanted to. He just couldn't.

He was afraid.

Charlotte shook her head, ran to the trap door, and climbed down. A moment later they heard the distinct sounds of her climbing up to the balcony. Then she laughed and stepped through the window.

In her arms was a ball of white fluff with black crumbs on his face.

"Buckets!" yelled Felix. "Why do you have black crumbs on your..." Felix's eyes got huge and he started to sniff. "Mint? No! Not the Thin Mints. No!"

Felix scurried out onto the balcony and returned a moment later with an empty box of Girl Scout cookies. "Since when can a cat open up a box of cookies? He doesn't even have opposable thumbs. Are you kidding me? For the love of Thin Mints, are you kidding me?"

Stanley was hardly even listening. He was still seated at the table, unmoving.

"You okay?" Charlotte asked.

He nodded. "But I think I'll head home now, after all."

CHAPTER SEVEN

JELL-O BREAKTHROUGH

The next morning, Stanley sat at his family's kitchen table. The sun streamed through the window and bounced off the wall. His mind drifted as he shaped his scrambled eggs into a circle and then flattened them.

"You thinking about actually eating that food sometime before school?" his mom asked. She was wearing her pink nursing scrubs and had her hair pulled back in a ponytail.

Stanley switched his attention to his hash-browned potatoes. He dug a little pit in the center of them.

"Earth to Stanley," his father said, wiping eggs from his freshly shaven face. "Your mom asked you a question."

"What?" Stanley said. "Oh, um, yeah. Sorry. Just thinking."

Stanley's younger sister, Rachel, spoke up. "Mom, why's Stanley always thinking about stuff?"

"Because," Mrs. Carusoe smiled, "Stanley is this town's premier detective, and he's caught himself an important case."

Stanley glared at his mother. "You're teasing me, aren't you?"

His mom smiled again and lifted a forkful of fruit to her mouth. "Not teasing. Encouraging," she said. "And by the looks of it, you could use some more."

"It's just all the data we looked at last night... it's so messy," said Stanley. "I can't make any of it fit."

Mrs. Carusoe exchanged a look with her husband. "Stanley, you know how your whole life, you've never, ever let the different foods on your plate touch?"

Stanley looked down at his plate. The eggs were in one corner. The hash browns in another. The toast had its own place, as well. At all points, the different foods were separated by at least a one-inch buffer zone.

"Well, Stanley," his mom continued, "sometimes foods get mixed up, and lots of times, things get messy. In life, not everything fits perfectly or easily."

"I know, Mom, but that's why I like math. Things *do* fit together perfectly in math."

His dad shook his head. "But that's just not true, son. Think about my job. I deal with numbers all day. Heck, as an economist, that's about all I do. I know how many jobs the country's gaining, what the stock market does, how the interest rates are doing, and the rate of inflation. And I have tons of data at my disposal—you wouldn't believe how much. But when I look at that data, my guess as to what will happen next might be totally different from the guess of the guy working at a different bank—even though he's using the same numbers I am. Numbers can get messy, Stanley, and when they don't fit perfectly... well, you just have to look for the best possible fit."

Stanley looked back down at his plate. "There's just got to be something I'm not thinking of." He flattened out his eggs and made them into a circle again.

"Stanley," said his dad. "Maybe there *is* something you're not thinking of. Maybe things do fit together if you just change your perspective and get a little messy." He made a sandwich out of two pieces of toast, some scrambled eggs, and half of his hash browns, then took a bite. "It's delicious."

"I. Don't. Like. Messy," Stanley said, as if to make the point for the last time. Then he flattened out his eggs and made them into a circle. Again.

*

Stanley followed the crowd into the lunchroom and took his usual seat near the center of the room. Charlotte was already there, and she had a funny look on her face.

"What's wrong?" Gertie asked as she joined them.

"I don't know. Just call it a funny feeling," Charlotte said.

"You mean a Stanley," said Gertie.

Charlotte winked. "Right, call it a Stanley. When I got here, the Science Club was in our spot. And when I came up, they all got really quiet, and Marie Shawl shoved something into her jacket real quick."

"Did you get a look at it?" Stanley asked.

Charlotte took a sip from her water bottle. "Just a glimpse. Not enough to make out anything definite. A bunch of lines and figures on graphing paper."

Stanley rubbed his chin. "Harry and Blaise were acting strange yesterday, too."

"Harry and Blaise always act strange," Gertie said.

"Yeah, but this was the 'we're up to something' sort of strange."

Gertie raised an eyebrow. "Are you thinking the Science Club could be responsible for the Mr. Jekyll crimes?"

Charlotte shrugged. "Hey, if kids are pulling these crimes, then we should keep an open mind about *everyone* in this school."

Just then, Felix sat down next to Stanley. His lunch tray was piled at least a foot high with green Jell-O cubes. He looked at his friends' skeptical expressions and said, "What? As if you aren't tempted to take a cubic foot of this stuff when you go through the line?" He grabbed a handful of cubes and tossed them into his mouth like popcorn. "So, what did I miss?"

"Charlotte got a Stanley," said Gertie.

"Congrats," said Felix. "What about?"

Charlotte shrugged. "I'm just keeping my antennae up for anybody acting suspicious, that's all."

"Like criminals using famous literary names?" Gertie said. "Let's not forget the obvious suspects here. Who else would choose something like Mr. Jekyll but the English Club?"

Stanley shook his head. "I thought of that. But the characters in that book are Dr. Jekyll and Mr. Hyde. No such person as Mr. Jekyll."

"And you know this bit of English trivia because...?"

"Polly and her gang don't have a monopoly on good books, you know."

Felix was bent over his plate now, slurping jiggling cubes directly into his mouth. He looked up. "I think it could be those Chess Clubbers. I just passed by their table and heard Sheba yell 'Queen to e5' while she moved her cheese stick next to Nick

Nickerson's raw broccoli."

"What does that have to do with our case?" Gertie said.

Felix counted on his fingers. "Playing chess with raw vegetables and cheese is weird. This Mr. Jekyll is weird. Lergo my ergo, I bet they're one and the same. Plus, they looked at me strange."

Green juice was dripping from Felix's teeth. Stanley, Charlotte, and Gertie all exchanged a look.

"And *that's* my cue to get more." Felix grabbed his tray and went back to the food line.

Gertie tapped her pen against the table. "You really think Jekyll could be someone here at school?"

"We do think it's a kid," Charlotte said. "Why not a kid from this school?"

"Well," said Stanley, "I need to go get my lunch. You girls want anything?"

They both shook their heads. "No thanks."

Stanley rose from his seat and turned away from the table just in time to see it happen. Felix was walking back to their table, his tray stacked high with Jell-O cubes. And as he walked past Dervin Chowder, Dervin nudged Felix just a little to the side—into Jack Pickle's outstretched leg.

It might not have been so bad if Felix hadn't tried to save his lunch. Off balance, he stumbled the length of the room, trying to regain his footing while not losing any of his precious Jell-O. But it was no use. Jell-O cubes flew left and right, and finally, with a loud crash, Felix, his tray, and the remainder of his Jell-O landed right in the lap of Gina von Gruben.

Stanley rose from his feet to help Felix—but when he looked down at the mess, he stopped. The green cubes were scattered all over the cafeteria, seemingly at random. And yet, they weren't entirely random. The path that Felix had walked formed a straight line through the chaos.

Something clicked in Stanley's mind. He thought about the map of Ravensburg and all those different Mr. Jekyll crimes. The crimes that seemed so random. And then it hit him. His dad was right. Sometimes, you can't find the perfect fit. Sometimes, you just have to find the *best* fit.

And while Gertie helped Felix to his feet, Stanley turned to Charlotte.

"I'll meet you guys at the treehouse after school. I've got a problem to solve."

CHAPTER EIGHT

LINE OF BEST FIT

"Hey, Felix," said Stanley, swinging open the trap door of the treehouse. "Sorry I left you in your hour of need."

Felix looked up. "Oh, a little old thing like getting humiliated in front of the entire school by Dervin? I'm sure you had better things to do."

"I said I was sorry. I needed to work on something."

Felix turned back to his tablet. "Well, you're not the only one working on important problems."

"Really? What do you got?"

Felix shrugged. "Oh, you know, only something that will change life as we know it *forever*. Get over here. You won't believe this."

Stanley raised an eyebrow. "You solved it?"

Felix winked. "Come witness my brilliance." He

turned his tablet around to face Stanley. "What do you see?"

Stanley stared at a long squiggly line that weaved through the southwestern part of Ravensburg. "Felix, what is this line? How did you do this?"

Felix smiled, dug into the right front pocket of his baggy jeans, and pulled out a phone. "With a little help from the CandyApp1000, invented Halloween morning, made famous right now."

"CandyApp1000? What does that have to do with Mr. Jekyll?"

"Mr. Jekyll?" said Felix. "Absolutely nothing. No, Stanley, I've been devoting this handsome brain of mine to more important matters today, like making next year's Halloween the most efficient night of candy reaping in history."

Stanley shook his head. "This isn't about Mr. Jekyll?"

"Just for a moment, could you start focusing on the serious problems of our world?"

"Like more efficient trick-or-treating?"

Felix pointed at Stanley. "Exactly."

Stanley sighed. "Fine, I'll humor you."

Felix tapped the screen and handed it to Stanley. "Invented by the devilishly handsome Felix Wonderbrain, the CandyApp1000 uses the GPS in my phone to track my trick-or-treating route."

"And how exactly does that help boost candy intake?"

"Every time I stop for more than twenty seconds at a time, the app records the location. Then, depending on the quality of treat, I rate it, and the app stores all of the information and sorts it out. For instance, Gertie and I made 72 stops this year, and our path is represented by this long squiggly line." Felix tapped the screen. "But based on how I rated those stops, I now get *this*."

He tapped on the screen, and it changed. The long line vanished and was replaced by three shorter lines. One path was green, one was yellow, and one was red.

"I'm not following," said Stanley. "The green line represents the path I'll take next year to hit all of the top houses on my route. I'm talking king-sized candy bars, wide selection, and signs that say, 'Take whatever you want.' The yellow path represents houses that are okay. Snack-sized candy with a small selection."

"And the red path?"

Felix shook his head. "No chance, partner. Those houses either have strict limits on how much you can take, or they have toothbrushes. Or maybe Almond Joys and Mounds bars. I have yet to meet someone who has ever eaten a Mounds bar. I heard it's actually reconstituted horse meat. Anyway, I was just transferring all this up onto the main map so I could plan what new houses to hit during the rest of the night next year. At this rate, in five short years, I'll have all of Ravensburg eating out of my hand. Or is it the other way around?"

"It's brilliant," Stanley admitted. "Also weird, ridiculous, and not at all helpful to us in the search for Mr. Jekyll."

The trap door popped open and Charlotte peeked through. "What about Mr. Jekyll?"

"If Mr. Jekyll was a bag of tropical fruit Skittles," said Stanley, "then Felix might have something. As it stands, I'm apparently the only one who did any real work on our Jekyll problem."

Gertie followed Charlotte up into the treehouse. "Not true. We girls did some after-school sleuthing of our own, trying to figure out what the Science Club is up to."

Stanley's eyebrows went up. "And?"

Charlotte stretched her arms over her head. "We've spent the last hour and a half in the public library, watching them. They sat there doing homework together."

"How do you know they weren't hatching their evil plans?" Felix asked.

"They were working out of their social studies textbook," said Gertie. "Probably studying for tomorrow's test."

"Though every once in a while Harry and Blaise would jump up and yell 'Nitroglycerin' and bump fists. That was a little odd," Charlotte said. "Anyway, I'm ready for some action. What do you got for us, Stanley?"

Stanley smiled. "Have I ever told you how much I love math?"

Charlotte and Gertie rolled their eyes in unison.

"Out with it, Genius Boy," said Charlotte.

"Well, you know how we were looking for some kind of pattern among the different points on our Ravensburg map?"

"Couldn't find anything," said Gertie.

"Correct. There was no pattern or relationship between the points themselves—certainly nothing that fit perfectly. But my dad's right. When things don't fit perfectly, you need to find the best fit possible."

"And?" said Charlotte.

"Well, duh—that means we have to find the line of best fit!" Stanley could hardly control his excitement.

"A line of best fit?" Charlotte said.

"Come on, guys," said Stanley. "You've heard of a line of best fit before."

Charlotte and Gertie both shrugged.

Stanley sighed. "Felix, you've heard of a line of best fit, haven't you?"

Felix was tapping away on his tablet computer. "Wait, what?" He looked up. "Um, that's that least squares regression stuff, right?"

Stanley's smile grew bigger. "Exactly!"

"Least squares regression what?" Gertie said. "Sounds complicated."

Stanley shook his head. "It's not that hard, really. When I thought about the map of Jekyll's crimes, it looked just like a scatterplot to me. Like a bunch of random points scattered across our map. And that reminded me of something I'd read about. Lines of best fit. Basically, a line that doesn't necessarily go through *any* of the points but gets fairly close to *all* of them."

"You've lost me," Charlotte said.

Stanley pulled a notebook from his bag and started writing. "Okay, let's say you've got five points on a graph. I've drawn the five points, and"—he drew a line—"here's a line that goes sort of between the five points. You see that?"

Charlotte and Gertie nodded.

"Good. Now what if I measured the vertical distance between each point and the line I just drew? That gives me five distances. Do you see that?"

They nodded again.

"If I were to square each distance and then add all those squared values together, I would get a number. Basically, what I want to do is find a line where that number is as small as possible. In other words, where the average distance between the points and the line is as small as possible. That is your line of best fit."

Gertie still looked uncomfortable. "This seems a little harder than the math we usually do."

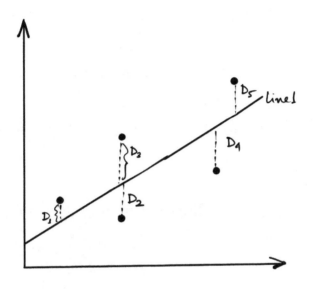

"Yeah," agreed Charlotte. "I'm still lost. How did you even come up with this idea?"

"It was Felix at lunch today," Stanley said. "The Jell-O incident. The line Felix left."

Felix raised a finger. "Oh, I get it! The Jell-O cubes were randomly spread out, but they were all close to the path I had traveled while I was stumbling. And that path formed a straight line."

"Oh," said Gertie. "Why didn't you just say that to

begin with, Stanley?"

"I thought I just did."

"So how does this help our case?" Charlotte asked.

"I've figured out the line of best fit for the Mr. Jekyll crimes." Stanley handed Felix a sheet of paper. "You think you can program this into your tablet?"

"Sure."

"Good, 'cause I think it's time to go see Officer Evans again."

CHAPTER NINE

A PRIME SUSPECT

This time when they sat in the interrogation room, Stanley and his friends were looking across the table at both Officer Evans *and* Chief Abrams.

Chief Abrams looked at each kid before letting his gaze settle on Stanley. "Evans here says you had a breakthrough?"

"Um, yes sir, Chief."

The chief unfolded his hands and opened them, palms facing up. "Well, the floor is yours."

Stanley nodded at Felix, who hooked his tablet into the projector and fired it up. An image popped onto the screen against the wall—a map of Ravensburg, with black circles scattered around.

"As you can see here," said Stanley, "we've plotted all of Mr. Jekyll's crimes on a map of Ravensburg.

At first, we tried to find a mathematical relationship to show why these fourteen crimes happened where they did, but nothing we came up with fit. And that's when we had a different idea. What if we don't need something that fits perfectly? What if we just need something that fits best?"

"I don't quite follow," said Chief Abrams.

"There is a concept in math known as a 'line of best fit.' Basically, it's used to find the equation of a line that fits data points the very best. Now, the equation for any line is given by $y = mx + b,$ where m equals your slope and b equals your y intercept."

Chief Abrams coughed uncomfortably.

"Sorry, Chief. Um, the equation of a line is pretty basic middle school math, and I remember during the last case you reminded me that the police *can* do math, right?"

Chief Abrams glared at Stanley. "Continue, please."

"I know what you're thinking," Stanley said. "How do we find the slope and the y intercept for a line of best fit? Turns out, we do it with these formulas."

Felix advanced the screen.

SLOPE = $[\sum xy - (\sum x \sum y)/n] \div [\sum x^2 - (\sum x)^2/n]$

Y INTERCEPT = $[\sum y - (SLOPE * \sum x)] \div n$

Chief Abrams and Officer Evans exchanged bewildered looks. The chief waved his hands back and forth. "Okay, you little smart aleck, I think you made your point with all your fancy formulas. So how about in English this time, so us non-Math Olympians can understand."

Felix stood. "I got this, Stanley. Let's say I broke into your secret donut room and drove away with a dump truck full of donuts. While I drove through town, a miniature hurricane started blowing donuts out of the back of my truck. When you went back and looked through town, at first, you'd think all of those donuts were scattered about at random, but after looking more closely, you'd see a relationship. A path."

"The donuts couldn't have gotten that far from where you were driving," said Officer Evans.

"Exactly. And the path I drove would be your line of best fit."

The chief looked at Stanley, then pointed at Felix. "See, that wasn't so hard."

Stanley sighed. "The point is, for the Mr. Jekyll crimes, this right here is your line of best fit."

Felix advanced the screen once more. It was the map of Ravensburg again, but this time a straight line ran from the southwest part through the northeast edge of town. The Mr. Jekyll crimes fell on either side of the line.

Ravensburg

Chief Abrams looked at the flat screen and scratched behind his ear. "I assume you're not suggesting Mr. Jekyll was driving a donut truck?"

"No," said Stanley. "Our guess is that Mr. Jekyll was trying to randomly pick his victims so it would be harder for police to find a pattern. But the thing is, it's really hard to be random. Even when people *try* to be random, they often do things in predictable ways. Our hypothesis is that Mr. Jekyll either works or lives along this line of best fit."

Stanley paused—and smiled.

"What?" said Evans.

"And… we found a very viable suspect."

"You did?" the chief asked.

Felix advanced the presentation once more. A star appeared in the middle of the screen, directly on the line of best fit.

Stanley pointed at the star. "We found someone who lives directly on the line—and he's one of the most horrible people any of us have ever met."

Felix advanced to the next screen—which showed a photo of a miserable kid.

Officer Evans practically choked.

"You know this kid, Bobby?" Chief Abrams asked.

Evans nodded. "All too well, unfortunately. He's

probably the biggest troublemaker Ravensburg Middle School has ever seen."

"What's his name?" Chief Abrams asked impatiently.

"Dervin Chowder."

The chief cocked his head and gave Evans a curious look. Then he turned back to Stanley. "Well, it's interesting, I'll give you that. But it's certainly not proof of anything."

Gertie crossed her arms. "Not proof? Dervin Chowder is the biggest psycho kid we know. He once replaced the teacher's room coffee creamer with powdered Alka-Seltzer. Poor Mrs. Friedman looked like she had rabies."

"And you heard Stanley," Charlotte added. "Dervin lives directly on that line of best fit."

Abrams cut her off. "All I heard was a fancy mathematical trick that led you four to conclude your least favorite person at school is Mr. Jekyll. If you've got actual proof, then let's hear it."

The kids looked at each other nervously.

"But—" Stanley said.

"Real, solid, evidentiary proof, the kind that

holds up in court," the chief said. "You find that, bring it in. Until then..."

"We'll find the proof," said Stanley quickly.

Abrams pulled his toothpick out of his mouth and pointed it at Stanley. "How can you be so certain?"

"Because," said Felix, "we're THE MATH INSPECTORS!" He jumped out of his seat and into the air, kicking out his arms and legs. When he came down, his leg caught the edge of the table, and he flipped completely over onto his back.

"Who exactly is this idiot?" Chief Abrams asked no one in particular.

"Ouch," Felix whimpered.

"Evans, do we need to lock this kid up?"

"No, Chief. Felix is just... a very strange human being."

"Thank you very much for noticing," Felix gurgled.

CHAPTER TEN

PROOF

"Well, if it isn't the Math Inspectors," yelled Dervin.

Stanley looked up. He and Felix had stopped at their lockers between first and second period.

As usual, the goons who hung out with Dervin chuckled. Jack Pickles was on his left, Jake Twinge was on his right, and Jackie Smythwacki followed behind. With one swift movement, Jackie kicked Stanley's and Blaise's lockers shut before moving down the hallway.

"Dervin and his Munions," Felix growled.

Gina von Gruben had the locker on the other side of Stanley. "Munions?" she asked.

"A cross between minions and onions," Felix explained.

"And why onions?"

"Because onions make me cry."

Gina looked to Stanley for help.

"They hung up his coat for him once," Stanley said.

"That doesn't sound so bad," said Gina.

"I was still in it," said Felix. "They left me hung up on the smelly old coat rack in the smelly old gym closet last winter."

Stanley patted him on the back. "He just dangled there, flailing his long arms and legs for three hours before I found him."

"They make me cry," mumbled Felix.

"Well. I'm no fan, either," said Gina.

"Yeah, I'm really sorry about that whole Jell-O thing," Felix said.

"It's not your fault." Gina looked down the hallway at Dervin. "And don't worry, someday all those guys are going to get what's coming to them. Eventually, what goes around comes around. We read about it in History Club all the time." She walked off to class.

"Well," Stanley said to Felix, "if Chief Abrams had taken our numbers seriously yesterday, we could all be doing without Dervin's presence today."

"Yeah. And his little Munions, too. Man, Stanley, when we were on our way to talk to the chief yesterday, I was envisioning our moment of glory. We would be by your locker this morning, getting ready for class and looking cool, when all of a sudden who would walk by but Dervin Chowder. And he'd be in cuffs and whining about his innocence. Officer Evans would be walking behind him, saying something like—"

"You can call your parents from the station," said a deep voice.

Stanley and Felix turned slowly. There, walking back down the hallway, was Dervin Chowder. In handcuffs. Followed by Officer Evans. Stanley and Felix were so stunned that they could only stare as Dervin was led out the main doors.

Finally, Stanley came back to reality and ran out the door after Evans. The officer had just finished putting Dervin in the back seat of his cruiser.

"Hey, Officer Evans! So, Dervin... he really did it?"

"Sure looks like it, wouldn't you say?"

Stanley hesitated. "But the chief said we needed solid, evidentiary proof."

Evans half-smiled at him. "You mean you don't know about the video?"

"What video?"

Evans got into his police cruiser and put a hand on the door to shut it. "It's the newest internet sensation— you shouldn't have much trouble finding it."

Stanley ran back inside. Apparently the others had gotten the news as well, because Felix, Charlotte, and Gertie had already gathered around, and Gertie was playing a video on Felix's tablet.

The video showed a dark scene, maybe just before sundown or just after sunrise. A large figure slowly came into focus. At first it looked like an alien. Antennae. Wings.

"Wait," whispered Stanley, "that's not... It is! But what's all over it?"

The light improved a bit, and Stanley could clearly make out the figure of a ten-foot-tall butterfly statue with what looked like squirming blue hair over its entire body. The video cut in for a close-up of the hair.

It wasn't hair.

It was caterpillars, hundreds of them, painted blue.

Then the camera panned down to the plaque at the base of the statue. Just beneath the words "Sunshine Magnet School Fighting Butterflies" was written the name "Mr. Jekyll." In blue paint, of course.

The video ended.

"Wow," Stanley said. "That's the creepiest thing I've ever seen in my life. But how does that implicate Dervin?"

"You didn't see it?" said Charlotte.

"See what?"

"Play it again, Gertie, but this time pause at the end."

She hit replay, and Stanley moved his face closer. And when she paused the video, Stanley saw what Charlotte was talking about. Reflected in the metal butterfly wing was the shirt of the attacker. The Superman symbol on the shirt was clearly visible, as were the words underneath it: "SuperDervin."

Dervin wore that shirt all the time.

"Wow, so he really did it," Stanley said. He was barely able to take his eyes off the screen.

Felix shrugged. "Guess he couldn't help going Jekyll on Sunshine Magnet School before the big rivalry game."

"Well, he's going to *miss* the big rivalry game as a result of this stunt," said Gertie. "Which means our chances of winning back the Crystal Chrysalis just went to zero. If you care about that kind of thing, I mean." She quickly added, "Which I don't."

Stanley looked thoughtfully at Gertie. "Come to think of it, why would Dervin risk missing out on the biggest game of the year for a stunt like this? Nothing means more to that guy than football. It's awful risky for him to videotape himself wearing his famous shirt, and then post it online. I don't know. It doesn't really make sense."

Charlotte put her hand on his shoulder. "Not this time, Stanley. No funny feelings about this one. It *was* Dervin. Not only did your math suggest it, and this video prove it, but when they took him, I saw a cop pull blue pens, blue spray cans, and blue markers out of his locker. Dervin *is* Mr. Jekyll."

"And I say we enjoy it," said Gertie.

"I'm with you," said Felix. "Off to music class in a Dervin-free hallway!" He took Gertie by the arm and skipped away.

Stanley shut his locker slowly.

Charlotte gave Stanley one of her looks. "Gertie's right. You need to enjoy this, Stanley. It's another case solved for the Math Inspectors."

"Right," said Stanley. "I'm sure you're right."

And he did enjoy it—a bit, anyway. Word that Dervin was gone spread like wildfire throughout the school, and almost immediately Stanley noticed something he'd never seen before in the halls of Ravensburg Middle School: smiles. Lots of them. Kids were happy. This was what real freedom felt like, and Stanley Carusoe, with the help of some beautiful math, was responsible for it.

By the time math class rolled around that day, Stanley was feeling pretty good about himself. Even Polly's sneer when she entered the room halfway through class didn't dampen his spirits.

But he knew something was up when Polly waved four hall passes in front of her so everybody could see them. They were red hall passes. Red meant somebody was in trouble. *Too bad*, thought Stanley.

As Polly walked over to Mr. Beagle, she looked at Stanley the whole time.

Mr. Beagle took the passes, hesitated, then looked over the top of his glasses. "Stanley, Felix, Gertie, and Charlotte, report to the principal's office immediately!"

CHAPTER ELEVEN

PRINCIPAL'S OFFICE

As they followed Polly through the halls, Stanley felt numb. He saw his legs moving, but he didn't feel them.

"Escorting people to the principal's office is not technically one of my duties as an office runner," Polly said, smiling. "It's more of a perk."

When they reached the waiting area outside the principal's office, Polly stared at them all for a moment. "Yes, this was every bit as delicious as I thought it would be. Take a seat, Math Nerds. Dr. Cooling will be with you shortly."

"Is this escort another part of the universal rules of fair play, Polly?" Stanley asked.

Polly laughed. "Even *you* must know the quote, Stanley. *All's* fair in love and war. Enjoy your visit."

Polly left, and Stanley, Charlotte, Gertie, and Felix were alone except for the muffled voices coming from inside the office.

"I've never been called to the principal's office before," Gertie said. "Felix, what's it like in there? And why are you grinning like that?"

Felix's face was frozen into a smile. "I think you guys need to rethink going to war with Polly. She just let me follow behind her without screaming at me once. And then she spoke of love. She's changed, I tell you—changed."

"Charlotte, wake him up," Gertie said.

"Ouch!"

Gertie pointed her finger at him. "We get called to the principal's office, you red-headed oaf, and that's all you can think about?"

Felix shrugged. "You guys worry too much. Trust me, this is going to be great. We just solved another mystery *and* got rid of the school's biggest bully all at once. Dr. C probably wants to congratulate us personally before all the news outlets want a piece of us."

Stanley sat up a little. "Do you think that could be right?" he asked the girls.

Before they could answer, the principal's door opened, and out came the last person in the world the Math Inspectors had expected to see.

Dervin Chowder.

And he was smiling.

"So long, math pukes," Dervin said as he walked out. His parents followed behind.

"Come on in," called the principal from his office.

When they went inside, they found another surprise: Chief Abrams and Officer Evans were already there.

"Sit down, sit down," said the chief as Officer Evans closed the door behind them.

Stanley looked from Evans to Abrams to Dr. Cooling. "I don't understand. You're letting Dervin go?"

Principal Cooling cleared his throat. His face grew serious. "I think you should sit down, Stanley."

"Not until you answer Stanley's question," said Charlotte. "Why *is* Dervin leaving?"

"Very simply," said the chief, "because he is not Mr. Jekyll. We dropped by to explain things to Principal Cooling, and we thought we'd have you four in for a little chat while we were at it."

Stanley shook his head. "But we saw the video."

Abrams leaned over the table. "And you saw Dervin's face on this video?"

"Well, no," said Gertie. "But we saw his shirt."

"Yeah," said Felix. "The SuperDervin shirt."

"He wears this shirt all the time, right?" Chief Abrams said.

"Yeah, it's like his master villain outfit."

"Which means everybody at school knows about it, right?"

"Yeah. So what?" said Felix.

Stanley was starting to get a very bad feeling about this.

"Well, it turns out that Dervin had an alibi for at least two of the Mr. Jekyll crimes. He and his friends were staying at his grandmother's house over in Lake Placid. No way he could have done them. So Officer Evans and I got to thinking. Evans told me how much trouble Dervin causes people. What a bully he is. And *I* got to thinking, I bet a guy like Dervin really likes to bully kids who love *math*."

Stanley felt his stomach tighten.

"And then I remembered," the chief continued, "that it was you guys who came down to the station with some crazy math proof pointing to none other than Dervin Chowder."

"You think *we* did this?" Stanley said.

"I think you've got motive. You're smart enough to frame somebody. And whaddaya know, now that you're the hotshot detectives helping out the police, you're in the perfect situation to do it."

"Come on, guys," Charlotte said. "We don't have to listen to this."

"Actually, you do," said the chief. "Because right now you guys are standing alone on the top of the suspect list."

"Okay, then let's hear the proof," Gertie said. "You said you needed proof before you would go after Dervin, right? So let's hear what proof you have on *us*."

The chief leaned back and folded his arms across his chest. "Tell me something. Who else in this school knows about Mr. Jekyll besides you four? Who else knows he tags things with blue paint? Who else knows he even exists?"

No one said anything.

"That's right," the chief continued, "nobody. So tell me this. If no one else even knows about the blue paint, who else in this school could possibly know to frame him by putting all that blue writing stuff in Dervin's locker?"

For a moment, they were all silent.

Then Charlotte said, "That's circumstantial, at best."

"So what does all that mean?" Felix asked.

Chief Abrams leaned forward. "It means you're downright lucky, because right now, all we have on you guys *is* circumstantial evidence. But while we can't yet *prove* you're responsible for any of these crimes, it would only take one small piece of hard evidence to do so—and the *next* meeting we'll be having will be down at the station."

They all squirmed uncomfortably.

Stanley shook his head. "But we helped you guys—"

"Some people might think that your help in solving the Claymore Diamond case made you grow too fond of being in the spotlight," Abrams said. "Some might suggest that you've now fabricated this whole thing for attention. Well, I hope you're happy, because you've got our full attention now, Math Inspectors. Or should I say... *Mr. Jekyll?*"

CHAPTER TWELVE

CAUGHT BLUE-HANDED

Stanley paced back and forth across the wooden planks of the treehouse floor. "I can't believe they think we did this."

"I'm not willing to trust Dervin's alibi," said Charlotte. "They *did* find all of that stuff in his locker, and we know *we* didn't put it there."

Gertie shook her head. "Listen, Dervin and his— what was that again?" She looked at Felix.

"Munions," he snarled.

"Munions." Gertie rolled her eyes. "Dervin and his Munions might be cruel idiots, but they *are* idiots."

"Your point?" Stanley said.

"My point is, we should have known from the start that he would never have been clever enough to pull off these pranks without being caught."

"So now what?" Charlotte said. "We start from square one?"

"There's no need," said Stanley. "My math was right. There's something we're just not seeing clearly."

Stanley stared at the map hanging from their whiteboard. He walked over and tapped on it. "Maybe trying to guess the suspect's identity is the wrong approach. Maybe it's time we look for a location."

"Meaning?" asked Felix.

"Meaning, go back to my original hypothesis that Mr. Jekyll is trying to be as random as possible—but that in doing so, he acts in predictable ways. The crimes are spread fairly evenly on both sides of the line of best fit. Except for right here." Stanley drew a circle around an area of town in the southwest of Ravensburg—an area where there were no black dots. "My guess is Mr. Jekyll will strike next somewhere in here."

Gertie, Felix, and Charlotte all studied the map and nodded.

"Makes sense to me," said Gertie.

A scratching sound came from outside the window, followed by a creaking.

Charlotte sighed. "Must be Buckets again. I'll go get him." She stuck her head out and looked around, then pulled her head back in. "Huh. I guess he left."

Stanley tapped the circular area again. "I say we patrol here tonight and hope Mr. Jekyll decides to pull another prank. You know what that means?" He pointed at Felix.

Felix rubbed his tummy. "Stakeout!"

*

The circular area the Math Inspectors had identified had a diameter of just under two blocks. In order to cover that much territory, they had to split up, and they had to keep moving constantly. They were equipped with walkie-talkies so they could each alert the others if they spotted anything suspicious.

Stanley tried to shake off his fear as he crept through the shadows. The moon was barely visible, covered by clouds that seemed to hang in the air like ghosts. A dog howled in the distance, and he jumped.

"Breaker, breaker," came a voice through the walkie-talkie.

Stanley jumped again.

The voice belonged to Felix. "This is the Skipper. Come in, little buddy."

Stanley pushed the talk button on his walkie-talkie. "First, I said radio silence unless you had something important. Second, since when did I become 'little buddy'?"

"Buckets and I watched a *Gilligan's Island* marathon last night, and well, it was either little buddy or Ginger. So, little buddy, while I've got you on the line, I thought this was supposed to be a stakeout. I've never moved so much in my life. This is more like a walkabout."

Charlotte's voice cut through. "A walkabout's what they do in Australia, Felix. Now would you please stop talking?"

"Fine."

The walkie-talkie went silent, and they continued their rounds.

But by 9:45, Stanley was beginning to wonder whether or not this was such a good idea. He felt good about his conclusion that this was Mr. Jekyll's next target location, but he couldn't be sure. And even if he was right, there was no reason to expect that Mr. Jekyll would strike tonight.

That's when he noticed a figure flash across the road, half a block away.

"Alert," he whispered over the radio.

"A burp?" Felix answered back in a loud voice.

"Not a burp," Stanley hissed. "Alert, suspicious movement in quadrant three. I repeat, suspicious movement in quadrant three. Request immediate backup."

"Which one's quadrant three again?" Gertie asked.

"It's coming toward Charlotte," Stanley said. The figure made a right at the intersection." Wait. It just turned, heading toward Gertie now."

Stanley quickened his pace to a jog, but when he came around the corner, he didn't see the figure. He stopped to look around. He noticed a wooden fence shaking back and forth.

He grabbed his walkie-talkie. "Gertie, the figure just hopped a fence and is heading your direction.

Sit tight and see if you get a visual on him."

"Or her," Gertie said.

Then Charlotte's voice crackled through. "I definitely just saw something, Stanley. I'm in pursuit."

Stanley looked at his map. "That doesn't make sense. Felix, where are you?"

"I'm backtracking, little buddy."

"Why, do you have someone behind you?"

"No, I dropped my Cool Ranch Doritos about a half a block back."

The wooden fence shook again.

What the heck? Stanley would have figured Mr. Jekyll was long gone by now.

Or—what if he was lying in wait?

Stanley swallowed hard. His body began to shake. He moved closer to the fence and pressed his ear against it.

Someone was definitely on the other side.

Then he heard a kind of hiss, like the sound a can of hair spray makes.

No. Not hair spray.

Spray paint.

Stanley backed away from the fence. "Felix," he whispered into his walkie-talkie. "Where are you?"

"I'm in major trouble, Stanley." Felix sounded scared—and not like he just dropped a Twinkie sort of scared. *Real* scared.

"What's wrong?" Stanley asked.

"I reached down to grab the bag of Doritos when a squirrel grabbed the bag."

"I'm sorry, Felix. But I need you here now."

"A squirrel, Stanley. I hate squirrels!"

Felix was too loud. Way too loud. The hissing from the spray paint stopped, and Stanley heard shuffling on the other side of the fence.

Then the fence began to wobble.

Stanley froze. He fumbled for his phone and dialed 911. But it was too late. A masked figure jumped from the top of the fence—right for him.

Stanley fell to the ground. Mr. Jekyll landed inches from his face, then ran off at a dead sprint.

Stanley was too scared to move. But he had to. He had to do something.

There was no point going after Mr. Jekyll, even if he could convince his legs to carry him—Mr. Jekyll was long gone. So instead, Stanley got to his feet and looked around. And on the ground, just where Mr. Jekyll had landed, Stanley spotted it.

A can of blue spray paint.

He bent down and grabbed it.

"Guys, I just missed Mr. Jekyll, but I've got his

blue spray paint."

Stanley saw the bright lights before he heard the tires screech. Police cars appeared out of nowhere and skidded to a stop in front of the sidewalk. The glare of the lights made it hard for Stanley to see, but he could hear a voice. A familiar voice.

"Stanley Carusoe, hold it right there and don't move." It was Chief Abrams.

Chief Abrams came from one police car, Officer Evans out of another. Evans looked at the can of blue spray paint in Stanley's hand. Then he looked up at Stanley's face and shook his head in disappointment.

Stanley knew how this must look.

Not good.

And then he saw that Evans was no longer looking at him. He was looking *behind* him—at the fence. Stanley turned around slowly.

In the light from the police cars, he could now see what he had been unable to see in the dark. Painted on the wooden fence was an enormous blue smiley face. And below it, in blue, were two words.

Mr. Jekyll.

Stanley turned back around.

He was in deep trouble.

CHAPTER THIRTEEN

RHYMES AND REASON

The Math Inspectors were placed in jail cell number three at precisely 10:33 p.m.

Charlotte's dad came to get her first, followed by Gertie's parents. Then Felix was picked up as well, and only Stanley was left.

Officer Evans shut the jail cell door and hesitated.

Stanley was trembling. "So just like that, we're arrested."

Evans shook his head. "I'm not going to lie to you, Stanley. It doesn't look good."

Stanley looked right into the officer's eyes. "Officer Evans, you've known me for a long time. I did not do this."

"It wasn't just catching you with the spray can in your hand, Stanley. We also found a note at the crime scene. I made a copy for you and your parents. Take a look."

The note was typed in fancy script.

OUR MODE IS TOO CLEVER BY ANY MEASURE;
WE MEAN TO CONTINUE THIS AT OUR LEISURE.

THE AVERAGE ABILITY OF RAVENSBURG'S FINEST,
WON'T RISE ABOVE MEDIUM—NOT EVEN THEIR WISEST.

WHEN MR. JEKYLL CAN STRIKE ANYWHERE, ANYHOW,
WHY IN THE WORLD WOULD WE HYDE NOW?

Evans looked at Stanley, expressionless. "Our analysts determined that Mr. Jekyll is more than one person. Notice the use of the plural pronouns 'our' and 'we.' And I'm sure you notice the words mode, measure, mean, average, and medium are all, well..."

"Math terms," said Stanley.

"Math terms indeed," howled Chief Abrams as he walked in behind Evans. "When I said we'd be meeting here at the station, I didn't expect it to be this soon. But I can't say I'm surprised. You kids got a big head about solving the Claymore Diamond case and were starved for attention, weren't you? So you come up with this Mr. Jekyll thing and start committing crimes." He pulled his toothpick out of his mouth and jabbed it at the air. "Crimes only *you* could solve. And along the way you probably think, 'Hey, this is a way to get rid of that kid who's been stuffing us nerds in lockers for the last few years.'"

A sudden thought occurred to Stanley. A terrible thought. "You thought we were Mr. Jekyll from the start," he said. "*That's* why you brought us in in the first place. You didn't want our help—you were just trying to get evidence on us!"

Chief Abrams grinned like a cat that had just swallowed a mouse. "Yes, I did, I'm proud to say. But let's let bygones be bygones. Tell me how you did all this without us catching you for so long, and I might be able to convince the judge to go easy on you."

Stanley clenched his jaw. He had nothing to say.

Another officer poked his head in the door and spoke to the chief. "Sorry to bother you, Chief. The kid's parents are here."

"Show them in."

Evans unlocked the cell door as Stanley's mom and dad walked in. His mom looked concerned, but his dad's face was hard as stone. Neither of them said a word to Stanley as they led him out of the police station and to the car.

But before Mr. Carusoe started the car, he paused, shook his head, and looked at Stanley in the rearview mirror. "I can't believe you're wrapped up in this. I'm so disappointed."

Stanley felt his throat tighten.

"Your mother and I have given you a lot of freedom to do, well... whatever it is you do with your friends. And to think *this* is what you've been up to?"

Mrs. Carusoe squeezed her husband's arm. "Henry, please."

"No, Clara. Our son was in *jail*. You heard the chief. This is serious." He ran his hand over his head.

"But Henry, Stanley didn't do this."

Stanley's dad made a face. "Oh, because no son of yours could possibly do something like this?"

Stanley's mom shook her head and reached out to squeeze her husband's arm again. "No, Henry. Because no son of *yours* could possibly do something like this. Don't you see? Stanley is just like you. He's curious, brilliant, and likes to solve problems... just like his father. And just like his father, he would never, ever do the things Chief Abrams described. Ask him, Henry."

Stanley's dad took a deep breath and ran his hand over his head once more. He turned around to face Stanley.

"Son, did you do this?"

"No, sir, I did not."

Stanley held his dad's gaze for a long, silent minute without blinking.

Finally, Stanley's dad sighed deeply. "I believe you," he said. "Do you know who *did* do this?"

"No," Stanley said. "I don't."

"Do you think you could figure it out?"

Stanley tried to sound confident. "If you give my friends and me the opportunity to look at everything again, with fresh eyes..." He nodded. "Yes, I can figure it out."

"Okay then, let's get you home so you can get a good night's sleep. You've got a big day tomorrow."

"What's going on tomorrow?"

"Tomorrow's your last day to figure out who this Mr. Jekyll really is. Because Saturday morning, the school board will consider a motion to see if you kids should be expelled."

Stanley couldn't believe his ears. "Expelled?"

His mother reached back and took his hand. "Stanley, you *need* to solve this case tomorrow. Like your father said, tomorrow will be a big day."

CHAPTER FOURTEEN

MAKE A SANDWICH

Stanley expected to be the first one to arrive at Felix's treehouse the next morning. He was wrong. When he popped open the trap door, Gertie and Charlotte were already busy at the whiteboard while Felix was working on his tablet.

"Hey, guys," Stanley said. "So... how mad are everyone's parents?"

Charlotte smiled. "My dad told me to find who set us up and rearrange his face."

Gertie took her pencil out of her mouth. "My mom said if we don't figure out who Mr. Jekyll is, she's going to throw my collectible set of horror movies in the trash."

Felix looked like he was going to cry. "And my mom said if I don't clear this up quickly, she's going to make me eat gluten free for a month. Gluten free, guys! I mean, my diet is 95% gluten. What on earth would I even eat?"

"Salads?" Gertie offered.

Felix whipped his head toward her and shook it slowly. "And I thought we were friends."

"Well," said Stanley, "I guess the good news is, our parents all believe we didn't do this. The bad news is—"

"Yeah, we heard about the expulsions," Charlotte said.

Stanley nodded. "So. Have you come up with anything yet?"

"Not really," said Gertie.

"How about you, Felix?"

"I think I've worked out the last few bugs in my CandyApp1000."

A marker hit Felix right in the forehead.

"Hey! What's the big idea?" said Felix.

"Felix Dervish!" Gertie screamed. "How can you possibly think of candy at a time like this?"

Felix stood up. "First of all, for your information, I can think of candy at *any* time. It's one of my best qualities. Second of all, I'm doing this for *us*. I figure if I can get CandyApp1000 on the market this morning, maybe sell it to some big firm by this afternoon, then we'll have enough money for a good legal defense... or enough money to bribe Chief Abrams to look the other way... or maybe we could move to Australia and have a walkabout."

Gertie shook her head. "So in your attempt to avoid going on a no-gluten diet..."

"That's right," said Felix. "I'm doubling down on sugar."

"Felix," Charlotte said, "You do realize that Mabel doesn't deliver to the prison?"

Felix's eyes went wide. "What part of good legal defense did you not hear?"

Stanley hardly heard this banter—he was too busy studying the map on Felix's tablet screen. There were no lines on Felix's candy map of Ravensburg, just the 72 different points representing the houses where he had stopped. They all looked completely and utterly...

"Random!" Stanley shouted.

The others exchanged a look.

"Stanley...?" Felix said.

Stanley studied the tablet a minute longer. Then he slapped his head. "I don't believe it."

"What? What is it?" Charlotte asked.

"You've got to be kidding me," said Stanley.

"Stanley Robinson Carusoe!" Gertie yelled. "Out with it!"

He sighed. "I think I might have royally messed this whole thing up."

"What do you mean?"

"Come look at this."

All the kids huddled around the screen.

"These dots represent all of Felix's stops on Halloween night," said Stanley. "If you didn't know anything except the dots on this screen, you'd think it was pretty chaotic. And if you thought it was so messy that it was best to find a line of best fit, then you'd probably have a line that looks a lot like this." Stanley dragged his finger across the screen from left to right.

"But then, if Felix told us that these dots actually represent the stops he made on the night of Halloween and showed us his path, well, see what happens. Felix, can you bring up that line?"

Felix hit a button, and one line showed up, connecting all of the dots in an improbable squiggly line.

"My line of best fit doesn't even come close to representing the real path that actually connects all of these events together," Stanley explained. He raced over to the board and erased his line of best fit. "Felix's impossibly squiggly line perfectly explains all 72 of his dots on Halloween night. What if there's a path or route that explains all of Mr. Jekyll's dots?"

"Like what?" Charlotte asked.

Stanley threw up his hands. "I don't know. Like, um, a bike path, or the path the mailman takes, or the phone company."

"Did you say mailman?" Felix said.

"Yeah, why?"

"Well, I told you my dad has maps of everything. He's got those kind of maps, maps that show mail routes, stuff like that."

"Felix," Stanley said. "Have I ever told you your dad is kind of weird?"

Felix smiled and headed for the trap door. "Gee, thanks for noticing."

A few minutes later, Felix returned to the treehouse with an enormous stack of maps he'd retrieved from his house. The Math Inspectors spread the maps around and started to compare any and all local routes with the locations of Mr. Jekyll's crimes. For the next fifteen minutes, the four friends studied the maps in furious silence.

Then Gertie squealed.

"I got something here. It's a bus map."

Stanley crawled over to see.

"A *school* bus map," Gertie said. "These are the bus routes for Ravensburg Middle School." She carried the map up to the whiteboard and clipped it beside the map of Mr. Jekyll's crimes. "Look at the route for bus number three. It hits five of Mr. Jekyll's crime scenes."

"Gertie's right," said Charlotte. "It's an almost perfect match."

"Yeah," Felix said, "but it may just be a coincidence. Bus number three doesn't go anywhere near the other crime scenes."

"Yeah, neither do buses one and two," said Gertie. "It could definitely be just a coincidence. What do you think, Stanley? You usually don't believe in coincidences."

Stanley took a long, deep breath. "Turns out Dervin living on the line of best fit might just have been one of those coincidences. But the bus path looks like it's the real deal."

"I can't believe we might actually wriggle out of this," Felix said. "We're ready for your command, boss."

Stanley put his hands in his pockets. He walked a few feet in one direction, then spun and walked a few feet in the other.

Then he remembered breakfast.

He looked up and smiled. "I think we have to make a sandwich."

"Now you're talking, Scoob," said Felix.

But Gertie didn't look convinced. "Um, how exactly will making a sandwich help us?" she asked.

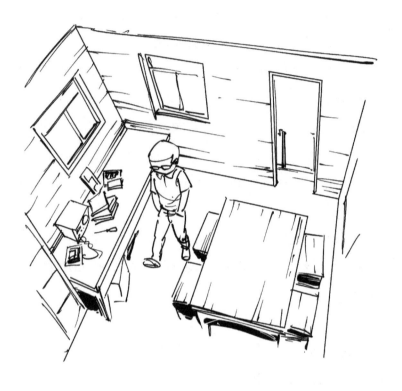

Stanley sighed. "I was so in love with my own math that I never let us investigate the crimes the way that, well, real detectives would. Maybe some things can't be figured out with math—or not *just* math, anyway. Maybe my dad was right. Maybe I need to get a little messy and make a sandwich—combine math with the good old-fashioned detective work I should have been doing in the first place. Maybe that's our best shot at finding Mr. Jekyll."

"You got a plan?" Charlotte asked.

Stanley looked at his friends. "Yeah, I've got a plan."

CHAPTER FIFTEEN

THE NEXT VICTIM

Stanley could feel people's eyes on him the moment he arrived at school. Word had clearly gotten around that the Math Inspectors were in big trouble. Fortunately, that uncomfortable feeling didn't last long, because ten minutes later something much more important became known.

Dervin was gone.

Not gone permanently, of course, but gone for the day. Word was that Mrs. Chowder was so troubled by the police's mistreatment of her son that she thought Dervin needed to spend the day regaining his self-esteem at the Love Yourself Day Spa. Stanley didn't know if the spa retreat was code for kicking puppies or stealing groceries from old ladies, and he didn't care. Everyone was so thrilled by Dervin's absence that everyone seemed to forget all about the Math Inspectors, and Stanley was able to spend the rest of the school day in peace.

Relative peace, anyway. There was still the matter of him potentially getting expelled from school. And when the last bell of the day sounded, Stanley felt that reality bearing down on him. He and his friends were running out of time.

They needed to solve the Mr. Jekyll case *now*.

And to do this, they would have to split up. Gertie and Felix were going to visit the five crime scenes that were located along the bus route. They would interview the victims of each crime and look for any potential leads. Meanwhile, Charlotte and Stanley had a bus to catch. The number three bus.

The first thing Stanley noticed when he and Charlotte boarded the bus was how crowded it was. There were three kids to each seat, minimum. He and Charlotte squeezed in near the middle, with Charlotte halfway on the end of one seat and Stanley immediately behind her.

Ethan Benish was squished beside Charlotte, and he gave her a big toothy grin as the bus pulled away from school. "This is great."

"Sitting on three inches of a bus bench is great?" Charlotte asked.

Ethan grinned. "When that three inches of bench is part of a Dervin-free bus? You betcha. I can't remember the last time I took the bus home."

Stanley leaned forward. "You mean most kids don't take this bus because of Dervin?"

Ethan nodded. "He and the Chowderheads have made the bus miserable forever. No kid in his right mind would ride this bus home while those guys are on it. Of course, today it's a little overcrowded because half the kids on here don't even live on the route. They just heard it was going to be a party."

In the front of the bus, Marcie Sidwell stood up and pointed out the window. "There they are!"

The bus exploded in laughter as they passed Jack, Jake, and Jackie—Dervin's Munions. They were probably the only kids living along the number three route who were walking home that day.

Charlotte turned around to look at Stanley. "Not too brave without Dervin, are they?"

After that, the noise level in the bus rose to a

fevered pitch. Kids were running up and down the aisles. Some were hanging out the windows. And even the driver joined in for a loud sing-along of, "100 More Days Without Dervin on the Bus."

Stanley leaned forward and whispered in Charlotte's ear. "What if Mr. Jekyll stopped taking bus number three because of Dervin?"

"Then he or she would be forced to walk home every day," Charlotte whispered back.

"And right past our five crime scenes."

Stanley and Charlotte kept a lookout and tagged each other every time the bus passed another crime scene. Ten minutes later, when they'd passed the fifth one, not a single kid had yet gotten off the bus.

Stanley turned to Blaise, who was sitting beside him. "Why isn't anybody getting off?"

"Are you kidding?" said Blaise. "This is going to be our last time to ride this bus all year long."

"We're on this thing till the end today!" added Gina von Gruben.

The kids around them erupted in applause.

And everyone really did stay until the end of the route. When the bus finally halted at its last stop, and the driver motioned for everybody to exit, Charlotte and Stanley watched the mass of happy kids disperse in various directions.

"Well," Charlotte said, "that wasn't a lot of help. Our lists of suspects just grew to seventy people."

Stanley sighed. "Hopefully Felix and Gertie can help us narrow it down a little. Let's start walking back."

Ten minutes later, they spotted Felix and Gertie riding toward them on their bikes.

"Hey, guys. I didn't think you'd be done interviewing the victims so fast," Stanley said.

Gertie and Felix exchanged a look.

"What?" said Charlotte.

"Well," Gertie said, "it may have something to do with the fact that I've never met a more miserable group of people in my entire life. They weren't exactly the social type. But I'm out of breath. Can we sit down and talk about this?"

"Sure," Stanley said. "So, what did you learn?"

"Two," Felix said. He rubbed his nose and held up two fingers. "Count 'em, *two* doors were slammed in my handsome face."

"Then Ida Rainey's dog, Mr. Booboo—" Gertie began, but Felix interrupted.

"More like Mr. Cujo. For a moment I thought I was a goner."

Gertie rolled her eyes. "All he did was nip you."

"It was a nip with intent to kill. That psycho dog squeezed through the fence and came after me before I could even get up to the front porch."

"But it's a Lhasa apso," said Charlotte. "He's not much bigger than a squirrel."

Felix started to shake. "Did you say squirrel?"

"Squirrel," said Charlotte with a maniacal grin. "Squirrel, squirrel, squirrel."

Felix yelped and covered his face with his hands.

Gertie shook her head. "Anyway, Henry Hood, the car mechanic? He didn't slam a door in our face—but only because he didn't have a door to slam. Instead, he spit a big loogie that hit my shoe."

"Well, that's four dead ends. How about the last crime scene?" Stanley asked.

Gertie looked at her pad of paper. "Ahh, yes, the enjoyable Mrs. Margaret Downing. Her son Julian threw a basketball that hit me in the head. Then

Mrs. Downing proceeded to tell Felix he smelled like armpit sweat, and she asked me if birds were making a nest in my hair."

"Wow!" Charlotte said.

"Yeah. And Stanley, I gotta be honest. At this point, I don't really care who Mr. Jekyll is. Those people are miserable, and they deserve whatever happens to them."

Stanley looked her in the eye. "What if I reminded you that finding out who Mr. Jekyll is might be the only way of keeping us from being expelled?"

Gertie sighed. "You're right. Let's nail the sucker."

"So you and Felix didn't come up with one piece of evidence, one observation, anything that might get us closer to the truth?" Charlotte asked. "Other than that all five of those people are mean?"

Stanley slapped his forehead. "That's it! Don't you see? All these people are miserable, mean, grouchy, you name it. *That's* what they have in common." He turned to Gertie. "Charlotte and I figured out that kids don't ride bus number three because of Dervin. Instead, they all walk. Which means they walk right past those miserable people."

"And Mr. Cujo," Felix added.

"Squirrel," Charlotte said with a smile.

Felix shuddered.

"So," Stanley continued, "just imagine for a second. Our Mr. Jekyll can't take the bus because of the meanest kid we know. He or she then walks home, only to be subjected to four mean adults and one killer squirrel."

Felix threw his hands in the air. "Okay, I've had about enough of the squirrel jokes! It may be small, but don't fool yourself. That Mr. Booboo has the eyes of a viper and the teeth of a great white shark."

Charlotte threw something to Felix, and he caught it.

"A cherry Blow Pop?" he said.

Charlotte shrugged. "Figured it would shut you up."

He unwrapped it and shoved it in his mouth.

Gertie tapped on her notebook. "Let's say you're right, Stanley. How does that help us figure out who Mr. Jekyll is?"

"Well, we're pretty sure now that it's someone

who was on that bus today."

"So, what? We put them all under bright lights until someone confesses?" Gertie asked.

Stanley shook his head. "We need to catch Mr. Jekyll in the act. For *real* this time. Which means we have to know where he's going to strike next."

"Yes, because that worked out so well last time," said Gertie.

Charlotte raised a finger. "But we know something this time that we didn't know before. For the first time, we know *why* Mr. Jekyll is committing these crimes. We know what the victims have in common."

"They're all mean," said Stanley, smiling. "Charlotte's right. All we need to do is find somebody really mean who lives on bus route number three. That's our best chance at finding the next victim."

"Then what?" Gertie said. "We just *hope* Mr. Jekyll commits another crime at that person's house tonight? And half of the crimes weren't even along this bus route. This is just a shot in the dark."

"You have any better ideas?" Charlotte asked.

Gertie shook her head and sighed. "Fine. So who's the next victim?"

Stanley shrugged. "Felix, can you bring up the map of Ravensburg on your tablet?"

But Felix wasn't paying attention. His head was up and his nose was sniffing the air. "Can't concentrate," he said. "Getting hungry, cherry Blow Pop not enough. What is that tremendous smell?"

Charlotte looked at her watch. "Must be Under Doggies. Mr. Under is probably getting ready for the dinner rush."

Gertie and Stanley looked at each other. "Under Doggies!" they both said in unison.

"It's right on bus route number three," Gertie said.

"And Frank Under is, without a doubt, the meanest man we have ever met," Stanley added.

"You really think Jekyll will go after Frank Under?" Charlotte asked.

Stanley nodded. "I think it's our best shot. Felix, how would you feel if I said 'stakeout' and 'Under Doggies' in the same sentence?"

"I'd say I feel like I could take on an army of squirrels. Let's do this thing."

CHAPTER SIXTEEN

FRAIDY CAT

Stanley walked by Old Milt's and shivered. *Why does Under Doggies have to be right by the haunted house?*

He surveyed the area. Mr. Under was more than a hot dog genius and master of insults. He was a paranoid who thought the world was out to steal his top-secret dog recipes—which was why he'd put up a twelve-foot privacy fence that surrounded the premises. Stanley's job was to man the front gate, and he had hidden himself in some bushes to do just that.

"Breaker, breaker." Felix's voice came over the walkie-talkie. "What's the 10-4 on whether Mr. Under will give us hot dogs for life after we catch this psycho?"

"What's the chances of you not thinking about food for once in your life?" Gertie hissed.

Felix, Gertie, and Charlotte had been patrolling the perimeter of Under's property for the better part of an hour.

"Guys, this could be all wrong," Stanley said.

"Maybe," said Charlotte over the walkie-talkie. "Or maybe we just need to wait longer."

"But we never did find a connection to the other nine crimes," Stanley said.

"They were probably miserable people, just like the ones Gertie and I tried to interview," said Felix.

"You're probably right, but why those locations? Bus number three corresponded perfectly to the five crimes on this route, but buses one and two didn't hit any of the other crimes. And those are the only buses that service Ravensburg Middle School."

Those other nine crime scenes had been bothering Stanley all evening. It just didn't make sense. If Mr. Jekyll was one of the students on the bus, what on earth could explain those other crimes?

He brought up an image of the map in his head.

Those other crimes were all in the northwest part of the city—near Sunshine Magnet School. It was almost as if...

It's almost as if two different kids at two different schools are committing these crimes.

That was it. That had to be it!

"I think I hear something," said Charlotte. "Stanley, it's coming your way. Repeat, coming your way."

Stanley froze and strained to listen. Sure enough, from somewhere along the fence line between him and Charlotte came the crackle of feet treading on fallen leaves.

He turned off his walkie-talkie. His heart beat wildly as he steadied himself by putting one hand against the fence. He remembered the last time he'd confronted Mr. Jekyll. His fear had allowed the criminal to get away. He couldn't afford for that to happen again.

He came out of the bushes and took three steps toward the noise, then stopped and listened again. Silence. No movement. Except...

Except the fence was shaking.

He snapped his head up and spotted a figure poised at the top of the fence. The figure wore black pants, black sweater, and a black ski mask. No doubt about it.

This was Mr. Jekyll.

Stanley tried to step into the shadows, but the figure had already seen him. It hesitated, as if torn about which side of the fence to jump down on. Then apparently it made up its mind... because it came flying through the air right at Stanley.

Stanley dove to one side, and the figure just missed him.

Mr. Jekyll jumped to his feet and took off.

Stanley yelled, "He's running! Mr. Jekyll's running!"

He took off after the vandal. Almost immediately, Charlotte appeared at his side and ran right past him. Then, up ahead, Felix and Gertie appeared from around a corner. They were right on Mr. Jekyll's heels.

Mr. Jekyll darted to his left.

Right for Old Milt's.

The others kept chasing him, but Stanley stopped. *Not Old Milt's. Anywhere but Old Milt's.*

Charlotte shouted over her shoulder as she ran. "Come on, Stanley, we've got to get him!"

Charlotte was right. Stanley kicked it into gear and gave chase.

"He went through a window!" Felix yelled. He held open the window, and Charlotte squeezed in first. Felix followed, then Gertie.

Gertie turned around. "You coming, Stanley?"

Stanley shivered, took a deep breath, then grabbed the windowsill and pulled himself inside. Felix and Charlotte were already halfway up the stairs of what was now an impossibly dark haunted house.

Stanley swallowed so hard, Gertie heard it. She turned around.

"It'll be all right, Stanley. We just stick together."

Stanley grabbed Gertie's sweatshirt and held on as she raced up the creaky stairs as fast as her stubby legs could manage. And just as they got to the top...

The haunted house came alive.

Smoke poured out of the floor, and a moaning sound came from the walls. A witch screeched, and eerie red lights blinked.

"He turned on the power," Charlotte said. "Be alert. He's trying to distract us."

Something cackled, and Felix dove at it. "I think I got him! I think I got him! Wait—okay, false alarm. It's just the head from a mummy."

A crash sounded nearby, and Felix shouted, "Get him, Charlotte! I'll be right there."

Through the flashing strobe lights, Stanley saw Charlotte tackle a dark figure trying to run past. Gertie ran to help, and Felix piled on too.

"We've got you, Mr. Jekyll!" Felix yelled.

"No you don't, Felix," said Gertie, "you've got me!"

"And both of you have me," growled Charlotte from below.

"He must have squirmed away!" Gertie yelled.

She tried to get up. But there was a problem. She couldn't. She, Charlotte, and Felix had all stumbled into a giant, sticky spider web. And now they were trapped.

"Go, Stanley!" Gertie shouted. "We're stuck in this stupid thing! You're the only one who can get him!"

"But I don't even know where he went," Stanley said nervously.

"He's getting away, Stanley! He's going to make a run for it, and there's only one way you can beat him outside!"

Stanley knew exactly what she meant.

The Tunnel of Death.

He looked toward the big, frightening mouth in the side of the hallway, and he lost his breath. He started to shake. "I—I can't."

"You have to!" Charlotte yelled. "Or would you prefer we get kicked out of school?"

Stanley looked once more at the black hole in the wall with its clown face and teeth dripping with blood.

I have to do this.

He ran directly toward the gruesome passage.

Closing his eyes, he dove into the gaping maw. He was too scared to scream. He was flung from side to side, shooting through the Tunnel of Death like a bullet through a barrel, holding his breath all the way. Then at last he was launched into the air, and he landed in the pit of Boogers and Vomit. He scrambled through the monkey heads and climbed out.

Just in time to see a masked figure running away from Old Milt's.

Mr. Jekyll.

Stanley sprinted after the figure. When he got close, he launched himself forward with everything he had and buried his shoulder into Mr. Jekyll's midsection.

He went down in a heap.

Mr. Jekyll howled as Stanley landed on top of him. The criminal started squirming, but Stanley wasn't about to let him go.

Stanley heard a commotion over his shoulder. He turned his head to see Charlotte, Felix, and Gertie running his way.

Charlotte's eyes were wide. "You got him?"

"I got him," Stanley said. He turned back to the figure squirming beneath him. "I give you... the mysterious Mr. Jekyll."

He grabbed the ski mask and tore it off.

The scared face of a small, familiar boy looked back up at them.

"Herman Dale?" Gertie squealed in surprise.

Herman's eyes darted around. "Would you get off me?" he growled.

Stanley climbed off as his friends circled around.

"Herman Dale?" Felix repeated, sounding just as surprised as Gertie.

Herman looked at each one of the Math Inspectors, then squarely at Stanley. "Why don't *you* look surprised?" he said.

"Because I finally figured it out a few minutes ago. Why'd you do it, Herman? You scared an awful lot of people."

"Not to mention, you had the whole town thinking we were criminals," snapped Gertie, still out of breath.

Herman's face hardened and he twisted his mouth up like a corkscrew. But he didn't say a word.

"If you don't tell us the truth, our next stop is the police station," Stanley said.

Herman shrugged. "I was just out for a nightly stroll when you guys chased me through Old Milt's haunted house. That's my story."

"Fine," said Stanley. "Have it your way. You know, for a long time, we thought there was no pattern to Mr. Jekyll's crimes, until Gertie here finally figured out that five of the victims lived along the route for school bus number three. Charlotte and I rode bus number three this afternoon." He looked at Charlotte.

She closed her eyes for a moment to review who was on the bus, then nodded.

"And you were on it," continued Stanley. "Then we figured out the reason Mr. Jekyll was committing these crimes."

Herman shifted his eyes just a bit.

"Mr. Jekyll was targeting people who had been mean to him," Stanley said.

"And dogs," Felix added. "Ferocious, man-eating, killer dogs."

Herman's shoulders dipped.

"So," Stanley continued, "we asked ourselves where Jekyll would strike next. And who's the meanest guy in Ravensburg? Frank Under."

Herman unfolded his arms, dropped them to his sides, and stuffed his hands in his pockets.

"But there was still a problem with our hypothesis," Stanley said. "The bus route only passed a few of the crime scenes. There were plenty more crime scenes that were nowhere near here. And as I was guarding Under's front gate, I was *still* trying to figure those out. That's when it hit me. What if those other crimes lay along *another* school's bus routes? Specifically, Sunshine Magnet School."

Herman began blinking rapidly.

"But the only way that would make sense is if a kid currently going to Ravensburg was once..."

Charlotte snapped her fingers. "A student at Sunshine, as well."

"Exactly," said Stanley. "*You,* Herman, were the only student on that bus today who used to go to Sunshine. *You're* the one responsible for all these crimes."

Herman was trembling now. "Do you have any idea what it's like to be picked on?" he said quietly.

Stanley nodded. "Yes, I do."

Herman's jaw set. "Every day of your life?"

Stanley hesitated. "No... I suppose I don't," he finally said.

"Well, it's horrible. And I just wanted all of them to understand just a little tiny sliver of the pain and fear I have to deal with because of them."

"I get it, Herman," Charlotte said. "Really. But you do realize you broke into people's homes in the middle of the night. I mean, that's pretty twisted."

"I know," said Herman.

"How'd you do that, anyway?" Felix asked. "Break into those homes and do that stuff without people waking up?"

"You really want to know?"

"No," said Gertie. "It's better that we don't know anything else. But there *is* something I'm curious about. I get all the people. I even get that miserable dog. But you also vandalized a water tower. What did the water tower do to you?"

Herman smiled. "That water tower serves our house. It's the worst water I've ever had in my life. That made me mad."

"Makes sense," Felix said.

Charlotte narrowed her eyes. "How about the fence? And why'd you leave that note with all those math terms?"

Herman looked honestly confused. "A fence? I don't know anything about a fence—*or* a note with math terms. Are you messing with me?"

The Math Inspectors stared at each other. Now they were confused, too.

Then Stanley nodded. "I should have figured that

out before. That note should have stood out like an improper fraction. Think about it: a poem that used math terms incorrectly? Well, well. So all's fair in love and war, huh?"

"I *knew* it," Gertie hissed. "I knew that good-for-nothing Polly Partridge had something to do with this! That note rhymed too well to be written by anybody other than an English snob. I bet she pretended to be Mr. Jekyll that night just so she could frame us for the crimes."

"But how would she have known we'd be out that night?" asked Stanley.

Charlotte punched her fist. "Simple: she followed us. You know those noises we kept hearing in the treehouse? We thought it was Buckets outside on the balcony. I'll bet you anything it was Polly spying on us!"

Felix stepped back. "You're saying Polly was spying on *me*? Me!"

"Doesn't even know you're alive, Felix," Gertie reminded him one more time. She turned to the others. "Charlotte's right. Polly spied on us, followed us, framed us for the crime, and then hoped we would get expelled. No, wait. She wanted more than just our expulsion. Polly Partridge wanted us to go to jail! Why, that little, no-good, Bob Shakespeare loving—"

Stanley cut her off with a wave of his hand. "Later, Gertie. Right now I want more answers. So Herman, here's something I don't get. Why the name Mr. Jekyll? The famous story is about Dr. Jekyll and Mr. Hyde. So why change it to Mr. Jekyll?"

Herman frowned. "Change it? I thought it *was* Mr. Jekyll. Huh. Must have messed that up. To be honest, I never was very good at English."

"I like you better already," said Gertie.

Stanley liked Herman too. He understood now why the kid had done what he did. Herman shouldn't have done it, but... Stanley understood. And he didn't want to see the kid go to jail. Unfortunately...

"Herman, we have a problem," he said. "We *could* go to the police and turn you in. But frankly, we've all been treated badly, and teased, and bullied, and... well, it doesn't seem fair to me that you should go to jail. On the other hand, it also doesn't seem fair that *we* should go to jail for something we didn't do."

"I'm sorry I got you guys in trouble," Herman said.

"I know you are," Stanley replied. "Which is why I've got a two-part proposal for you. First off, I want you to promise me you'll stop pulling these Mr. Jekyll crimes. You're finished. That's it. And instead of getting angry and wanting revenge on people all the time, instead... well, I'd invite you to hang out with friends."

"But I don't have any friends," said Herman.

Stanley exchanged a look with Charlotte, Felix, and Gertie. "You do now."

"You're serious?" Herman said.

"I'm serious," said Stanley.

Herman looked like he didn't know what to say. "Thanks."

Stanley shrugged. "Come to think of it, having a guy around with talents like yours may even come in handy."

"You said a two-part proposal," Herman said.

"What's the second part?"

"The second part," Stanley said, "is actually the first part. *Before* you stop pulling these crimes... I want you to pull one more caper. For us."

Herman's eyes widened. "You want me to get Under Doggies? I would love that. I could spray paint his head blue. I could paint all of his hot dogs blue. Heck, I could superglue his hands together."

"But that doesn't have anything to do with the color blue," said Felix.

Herman smiled. "I know. But it would be really awesome."

"No," said Stanley, "I don't want you to do anything to Mr. Under. I have a very different victim in mind."

Gertie raised an eyebrow. "Are you thinking of who I think you're thinking of?"

Stanley smiled. "Like she said, all's fair."

CHAPTER SEVENTEEN

ONE LAST JOB

The next morning at eleven a.m. sharp, Stanley, Charlotte, Gertie, and Felix, all of them dressed in their best clothes, were seated in the front row of the school board meeting. Their parents sat behind them.

"All rise," said Mrs. Lumpus, director of the school board, as she led the members into the room.

"Good grief," said Gertie. "Who do they think they are?"

"Hold it together, Gertie," Stanley whispered. "We have to play along. The rest is out of our hands."

Gertie nodded at the board members. "This isn't exactly stacked in our favor."

Stanley knew what she meant. Dervin's dad and

Polly's mom were two of the five board members, and he was pretty sure they weren't going to go out of their way to come to the defense of the Math Inspectors.

After the pledge, Director Lumpus led the board in all three verses of the Ravensburg Public School District song. Finally, everyone in the room sat down and a projector screen revealed the agenda. The Math Inspectors' case was third in line.

Stanley looked at his watch. It was going to be close.

Director Lumpus sounded her gavel for silence. "First order of business: an emergency item has been added at the last minute. Mr. Chowder, would you proceed, please?"

"Certainly, Director. As everybody in this room knows, the Caterpillars were destroyed by the Butterflies in last night's game. And everybody in this room also knows it's solely because my son, Dervin, was unable to play in the game due to an allergic reaction he had to his spa treatment yesterday morning."

Mr. Chowder held up a pad of paper. "I have here

one hundred signatures asking this board to intervene. We, the petitioners, are asking for a do-over as soon as Dervin's skin heals. Please, fellow members of the board, return the Crystal Chrysalis to its rightful home. Let the kids play again!"

"Thank you, Mr. Chowder," said the director. "We will put the issue to a vote."

Stanley looked at his watch again. Every minute counted.

One by one, each member of the school board stated aloud their vote on Mr. Chowder's proposal. Not surprisingly, the votes followed school lines: Mr. Chowder and Mrs. Partridge, both from RMS, voted in favor of the proposal, while the other three members of the school board, who were all from Sunshine Magnet School, voted against. The proposal was denied, and as a result, the Butterflies were declared Rivalry Champions for the year.

Director Lumpus had to use her gavel several times to quiet the room for the next agenda item. "Would the RMS Science Club please approach the podium?"

Stanley looked around in surprise. There, in the

back of the room, sat Blaise Brown, Harry Mendel, Jerome Baxter, and Marie Shawl. He'd almost forgotten about them. They had been acting suspicious lately. Now maybe he'd figure out why.

They walked to the front and faced the board.

Blaise cleared his throat. "After much research, it has come to our attention that there is too much waste at Ravensburg Middle School. We, my fellow Science Club Members and I, have painstakingly created a system to increase our school's recycling by 94%. It's so new, and it will clear out so much waste, that we've named it the New-Clear Waste Management Program. Our plan is less than a hundred pages long, so it shouldn't take long for you all to read, but we feel confident..."

Stanley felt his attention begin to wander. *This* was what all the Science Club's secrecy had been about?

As Blaise droned on, Stanley zoned out. He didn't even realize the meeting had moved on until the gavel sounded again and those dreaded words came.

"Would the four students calling themselves 'The

Math Inspectors' please stand?"

They stood. Stanley felt every eye in the room staring at the back of his head.

"And now," said Director Lumpus, "we call forth Chief Abrams of the Ravensburg Police Department. Keep in mind, fellow members of the board, these four children are going to be dealt with by the law for serious crimes of vandalism. Today, we are gathered to decide whether to expel them as they await trial."

Stanley swallowed hard and looked at his watch. *Felix had better be right,* he thought.

Chief Abrams walked the school board through the particulars of the case. Mr. Chowder and Mrs. Partridge stopped him at times to ask why he thought certain aspects of the case incriminated the Math Inspectors, and each time Chief Abrams took the time to explain.

When he finished, Director Lumpus shook her head in disappointment. Then she looked directly at Stanley. "Mr. Carusoe, we are very fair people, and we want to give you every chance to defend yourself. What do you have to say?"

Stanley looked at his watch for what had to be the tenth time. Then he began.

"Dear esteemed members of the board. I had hoped that our exemplary record—as students and citizens who helped uncover an injustice—would have worked in our favor. But I can see it has not. Despite the evidence that Chief Abrams presented, all I can do is look you straight in the eyes and tell you this: I am the son of Henry and Clara Carusoe, and I swear to you, by everything that that means to me, that my friends and I did not do these things.

"But, since I don't think that my word is going to be enough for you, I will attempt to offer you the only proof of our innocence I can think of. Ladies and gentlemen of the board, I give you... Felix Dervish."

Felix stepped forward. "A true problem came into my life on Halloween night," he said. "But I didn't know it until the next day. There I was, sitting on my floor, staring at two piles of candy. One was malt balls. The other was cherry lollipops. In some random freak of Halloween luck, over half of my candy lay in those two piles."

Mrs. Partridge sneered. "I fail to see what that has to do with the present situation."

"And how does a six-foot kid still get anyone to give him candy on Halloween?" asked another board member.

"An excellent question," Felix said, "and I promise to make it all as clear as mud in just a few minutes, if you'll let me continue."

Stanley surreptitiously signaled Felix to stretch the presentation as much as he could.

"But don't be worried," Felix said. "I went down to the fridge to think things over with a jar of dill pickles. And that's when I had my breakdown—I mean break*through*. I call it the Maltdillpop. Part chocolate malt, part pickle, part lollipop—and all amazing. Mabel has agreed to serve them on a trial basis."

"I'm going to have to put a stop to this..." began Director Lumpus.

"Let them speak!" bellowed a voice from the back of the room. Coach Bellum. Clearly the Maltdillpop had Coach intrigued.

"Yeah," said Felix, "I haven't even gotten to the

Hoinkie Float. A Twinkie, stuffed inside a Ho Ho, nestled in a mug of root beer."

"Enough!" roared Lumpus. "I think we have all we need to hold a vote. We will take the traditional five minutes of deliberation."

Mrs. Partridge leaned toward her microphone. "I don't think we need those five minutes, Director. I say we give our votes now."

The other board members nodded in agreement.

"Very well," said Lumpus. "I will give mine last."

She pointed at each member in turn.

"Mr. Smith?"

"Expel."

"Mr. Chowder?"

"Expel."

"Ms. Grossman?"

"Expel."

"Mrs. Partridge?"

"Expel them."

"Well," said Director Lumpus. "I can see it's not necessary for me to vote. But I want to set a strong precedent for justice. And that's why I vote—"

Just then, Mrs. Partridge's phone rang. Instead of

silencing it, she answered in a hiss. "You know Mommy's busy. This had better be important!" She paused, then all of a sudden she shrieked and stood up. "*What?*"

Mrs. Partridge stumbled away from the school board table and started running down the aisle toward the exit. "Don't worry, Poopsie, Mommy's coming!" she shouted into the phone.

"Mrs. Partridge!" Lumpus yelled. "What happened?"

Mrs. Partridge spun around. "It's that Mr. Jekyll monster. He just struck again. Just this minute! He got my poor Polly!"

The whole room gasped.

Chief Abrams looked down at his phone. "Well, I'll be..." He snapped his head up at the school board. "I've got an emergency." He started to walk away.

Then he stopped and looked at Stanley and the others. He frowned, then turned back to the school board. "But if Mr. Jekyll struck while these kids were here, then... well, these four obviously can't be Mr. Jekyll. All charges will be dropped."

*

With Chief Abrams's decision, the school board members had no choice but to change their votes. The Math Inspectors would not be expelled after all. And as soon as the meeting was adjourned, the four friends and their parents went to Mabel's diner to celebrate with some Maltdillpops.

After one taste, everyone agreed the invention was as obnoxious and disgusting as they had imagined. Well, everyone except for Felix. He was so satisfied, he ordered everybody a round of Hoinkie Floats as well. And nobody really minded. Because, as it turned out, Felix's strange fascination with Polly had finally come in handy. Somehow, Felix had known that at eleven a.m. every Saturday, Polly and her friends liked to dress up and practice Shakespeare plays in her back yard.

And that knowledge had been key to the plan.

When the gang left Mabel's and returned to the treehouse, Felix immediately pulled out his tablet. He located an internet video that had already received a surprising number of views. "Looks like Herman's already uploaded it," he said, then sighed.

"This is going to hurt me more than you, Polly."

He pressed play on the video.

The camera bounced as it moved along the roof of a white two-story house. It was focused on a back yard where several twelve-year-olds in strange outfits were practicing a play. The camera zoomed in on one of the girls: Polly Partridge. She seemed to be lost in the brilliance of her own performance.

She leaned dramatically on a rope that hung from a window above her makeshift balcony and said passionately, "Romeo, Romeo, wherefore art thou, Romeo?"

The camera held steady as an avalanche of blue paint came pouring out of a bucket tied to the rope— and splashed right onto the head of the fair Juliet. The now very blue Polly Partridge screamed her head off.

"That's gonna leave a mark," said Gertie.

"A very blue mark," Charlotte agreed. "Herman used heavy-duty paint. She'll be scrubbing for weeks."

The camera then panned to the front yard, where a name was written on the lawn in large blue letters.

Mr. Jekyll.

The video ended, and the four Math Inspectors gave each other high-fives.

Then Felix picked up the TV remote control. "Let's see what our old pal the chief has to say." He changed the channel to Stella Burger's *Five O'Clock Rock.*

"Well, no, Stella," Chief Abrams was saying, "we

don't have any leads. But we *are* reopening the case into the criminal mastermind known as Mr. Jekyll, and we are confident we will uncover his real identity soon."

"Wrong again, Chief," Stanley said to the TV. "Because Mr. Jekyll is officially retired."

"Besides," said Felix, "if you want a case solved, you go to... THE MATH INSPECTORS!" He jumped up from the couch and stuck out his arms and legs. This time—finally—his multiplication sign went off perfectly and he landed on his feet.

Stanley laughed. "You're still a very strange human being, Felix Dervish."

Felix smiled. "Thanks for noticing."

CHAPTER EIGHTEEN

MEANWHILE

When all the other businesses in town shut their doors for the evening, the lights of the shop turned on.

Skilled hands made exact marks and precise cuts on carefully chosen wood. By three a.m., another prototype was finished.

It met the construction requirements. It maneuvered with pinpoint accuracy. But would it pass the final test?

A number of seventy pound bags of sand were piled onto it. It held strong.

"One more," said the craftsman, putting the final sandbag in place.

For a moment, it looked like everything had worked. The prototype held.

Then it groaned loudly and collapsed into a pile of splintered wood.

The craftsman sighed and looked at the clock, then at the calendar.

Forty-seven days left.

While the people of Ravensburg slept on, the jagged fragments were swept into a pile. Then the craftsman carefully chose another piece of wood and pulled out the plans for the next version of the prototype. Time was running out, and too much was riding on this order to even think of sleep.

That was the cost of doing business with the Boss.

END OF BOOK TWO

BONUS MATH PROBLEMS...

Do You Have What It Takes
To Be A Math Inspector?

GERTIE: *Hey, everybody, Gertie here! Stanley promised I wouldn't be stuck making up all of the word problems again—but of course that's exactly what happened. What a shock! Charlotte and her dad are on a hunting trip, and Stanley and his dad are visiting the Hudson Valley Museum of Counting By Five (or something like that), And Felix... well, he has no good excuse to duck out of this. It's okay, though, I've got you covered. After all, this is important. Keeping your math skills sharp is what every good Math Inspector does. Wait a second, what's that smell? It smells like something's burning, like zombie flesh or something. Whoa! That would be so cool if it was zombie flesh. I'd better go check on Felix. But here's a problem to get you started. Gertie out!*

Word Problem #1 – Let's say that the meanest (and did I mention smelliest?) man in the world, Frank Under, sells 500 hot dogs on a typical Friday night in October. If Under Doggies is only open for 7.5 hours on Friday night, then how many hot dogs does Mr. Under sell per hour?

FELIX: *Hey, dudes. Short Stuff over here is trying to put out a tiny, insignificant fire. Turns out—yeah, Gertie? Yes, I called you Short Stuff. No, I don't want you to kick me in the shins. No, I will never call you short again. Can I call you vertically challenged instead? Okay, guys, by the looks of the steam pouring out of her nostrils, I think Short Stuff—er, Gertie—is really mad at me. Anyway, while she finishes putting out the fire and calming down, I'd better give you one of my famous word problems.*

Word Problem #2 – Let's say, hypothetically, that the prettiest girl in school leaves a note in some handsome tall kid's locker. And in this note, she cleverly disguises her phone number with an almost unbreakable code. How exactly would you go about cracking that—

GERTIE: *STOP, STOP, STOP! Felix, what the heck do you think you're doing? Let me see that code. Felix! This note says RATFACE.*

FELIX: *Attention everybody! Short Stuff here has just proven that she can read. Of course it says RATFACE. I was just getting to that before I was so rudely interrupted. I thought our readers could help me break this code so I could figure out Polly's phone number.*

GERTIE: *Incredible. You know what, Felix? I think our readers need to turn their heads because this is about to get violent. FELIX DERVISH! This is not a code, this is a note calling you a RATFACE. Polly does not like you. She will NEVER like you. Now, please, forget about Polly Partridge and come up with a math problem for everybody.*

FELIX: *Well, that was just plain mean and I feel like I want to cry. I sort of wish Buckets was here... but I won't cry. Not now. Instead, Miss Vertically Challenged, we'll do it your way. I'll just give our readers a problem inspired by my latest cooking project.*

GERTIE: *You mean the one that just caught on fire?*

FELIX: *A point of clarification, it only partially caught on fire. The rest of my famous concoction for my annual Halloween-I-Miss-You Party is just fine.*

GERTIE: *Is that dirt stew?*

FELIX: *Nope, it's chocolate soup.*

GERTIE: *That's disgusting, and therefore I'm intrigued. Are those eyeballs?*

FELIX: *Technically they're marshmallows with raisins jammed into the middle of them. And the worms are gummies. And you should see what else is in here, although I do wait to put the Butterfingers in till the very end so they melt just enough to look like—*

GERTIE: *Please stop talking before everybody throws up in their books. Can you just give the readers a real math problem now?*

FELIX: *Such a fun-killer. Okay, dear reader, after years of experimentation, I finally discovered the precise ratio of ingredients that makes my Chocolate Eyeball Soup a masterpiece. See if you can use that ratio to figure out this next problem.*

REAL Word Problem #2 – If my secret Chocolate Eyeball Soup recipe calls for a 4:1 ratio of milk to melted chocolate, and I'm using 5 gallons of milk for this batch, how many gallons of melted chocolate do I need?

GERTIE: *Um, Felix, do you have any problems that don't include either Polly or food?*

FELIX: *That's like asking if you have any shoes that make you look tall. In other words, not a chance. Here's the next problem.*

Word Problem #3 – Let's further suppose that Mabel decides to start selling jars of my gourmet Chocolate Eyeball Soup. If I decided to make 5.5 gallons of soup, and I put them in one-pint jars, how many jars would I need?

GERTIE: *Felix, we get it, okay? Math is handy when it comes to filling your stomach, but maybe you should pay more attention to what you're doing. It looks like you had an eyeball fall over the side of the pot there. It landed on the burner. Okay, now it's in flames. Is that what happened last time? How about you put the fire out this time and I'll give our readers a real problem?*

Word Problem #4 – Let's say that the human shoulder stops functioning after being hit 215 times in a row. Let's say I punch Felix in the shoulder 37 times per hour. At that rate, how many minutes will it take before his shoulder stops working?

GERTIE: *Thanks, readers, as always. Now, while you try to figure out that answer on paper, I'm going to go conduct what I'd like to call a live experiment. Gertie out!*

To check your answers or to learn more about The Math Inspectors, go to www.TheMathInspectors.com.

GET TWO DANIEL KENNEY STORIES FOR FREE

BUILDING A RELATIONSHIP WITH MY READERS IS THE VERY BEST THING ABOUT WRITING. I OCCASIONALLY SEND NEWSLETTERS WITH DETAILS ON NEW RELEASES, SPECIAL OFFERS, AND OTHER BITS OF NEWS RELATING TO THE MATH INSPECTORS AND MY OTHER BOOKS FOR KIDS.

AND IF YOU SIGN UP TO THIS MAILING LIST, I WILL SEND YOU THIS FREE CONTENT:

1. A FREE COPY OF MY PICTURE BOOK, *WHEN MR. PUSH CAME TO SHOVE.*
2. A FREE COPY OF MY HILARIOUS ILLUSTRATED BOOK FOR YOUNG PEOPLE, *THE BIG LIFE OF REMI MULDOON.*

YOU CAN GET BOTH BOOKS FOR FREE, BY SIGNING UP AT WWW.DANIELKENNEY.COM.

DID YOU ENJOY THIS BOOK? YOU CAN MAKE A BIG DIFFERENCE!

REVIEWS ARE THE MOST POWERFUL TOOL IN MY ARSENAL WHEN IT COMES TO GETTING ATTENTION FOR MY BOOKS. MUCH AS I'D LIKE TO, I AM NOT A BIG NEW YORK PUBLISHER AND I CAN'T TAKE OUT FULL SIZE ADS IN THE NEW YORK TIMES OR GET MYSELF A SPOT ON NATIONAL TELEVISION SHOWS.

BUT I AM HOPING THAT I CAN EARN SOMETHING MUCH MORE POWERFUL THAN THOSE THINGS. SOMETHING THE BIG PUBLISHERS WOULD LOVE TO HAVE.

A COMMITTED AND LOYAL BUNCH OF READERS.
HONEST REVIEWS OF MY BOOKS HELP BRING THEM TO THE ATTENTION OF

OTHER READERS. IF YOU'VE ENJOYED THIS BOOK, I'D BE VERY GRATEFUL IF YOU COULD SPEND JUST FIVE MINUTES LEAVING A REVIEW (IT CAN BE AS SHORT AS YOU LIKE) ON THE BOOK'S AMAZON PAGE.

THANK YOU VERY MUCH!

THE MATH INSPECTORS BOOKS

BOOK ONE: THE CASE OF THE
CLAYMORE DIAMOND

BOOK TWO: THE CASE OF THE
MYSTERIOUS MR. JEKYLL

BOOK THREE: THE CASE OF THE
CHRISTMAS CAPER

BOOK FOUR: THE CASE OF THE
HAMILTON ROLLER COASTER

BOOK FIVE: THE CASE OF THE
FORGOTTEN MINE
COMING SOON!

ALSO BY DANIEL KENNEY

THE SCIENCE INSPECTORS SERIES
COMING SOON!

THE HISTORY MYSTERY KIDS SERIES

THE PROJECT GEMINI SERIES

THE BIG LIFE OF REMI MULDOON

TEENAGE TREASURE HUNTER

KATIE PLUMB & THE PENDLETON GANG

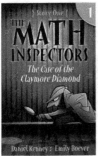

When the Claymore Diamond is stolen from Ravensburg's finest jewelry store, Stanley Carusoe gets the bright idea that he and his friends should start a detective agency.

Armed with curiosity and their love for math, Stanley, Charlotte, Gertie and Felix race around town in an attempt to solve the mystery. Along the way, they butt heads with an ambitious police chief, uncover dark secrets, and drink lots of milkshakes at Mabel's Diner. But when their backs are against the wall, Stanley and his friends rely on the one thing they know best: numbers. Because numbers, they never lie.

Sixth-graders Stanley, Charlotte, Gertie and Felix did more than just start a detective agency. Using their math skills and their gut instincts, they actually solved a crime the police couldn't crack. Now the Math Inspectors are called in to uncover the identity of a serial criminal named Mr. Jekyll, whose bizarre (and hilarious) pranks cross the line into vandalism.

But the deeper the friends delve into the crimes, the more they realize why they were asked to help...and it wasn't because of their detective skills.

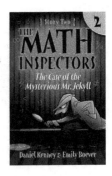

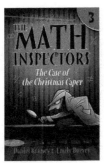

It's Christmas Eve in Ravensburg, and the town is bursting with anticipation for its oldest Christmas tradition. The annual opening of Douglas and Son's Toy Store, home of the greatest toys in the world, is finally here. But this is no ordinary Christmas Eve, and the surprise that awaits them is beyond any of their wildest imaginations: a surprise that threatens to ruin Christmas!

Stanley, Charlotte, Gertie and Felix call in a little backup, but will the team's detective skills and math smarts be enough to unravel the mystery?

Summer vacation has finally arrived, and the Math Inspectors deserve a break. After all, their sixth-grade year was a busy one. On top of all the normal school stuff, Stanley, Charlotte, Gertie, Felix, and Herman made quite a name for themselves as amateur detectives. But when a relaxing day of roller coasters, riddle booths, and waffle eating contests turns into a desperate scramble to save a beloved landmark, the friends quickly discover that this case may be asking more than they are willing to give.

In fact, there may only be one way out—to quit. Will this be the end of the Math Inspectors?

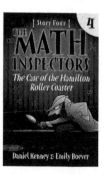

Where did Professor Abner Jefferson go? Before they can find out, April, Henry, and Toad find themselves transported back in time to colonial Florida. Now they have to figure out what's going on, where their father is, and how to get home. Can they find the missing pieces to the puzzle or will they be stuck in history forever?

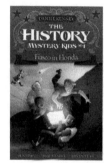

The History Mystery Kids 1: Fiasco in Florida is the first book in an exciting new time travel series meant for children who have already been reading chapter books and are ready for something more advanced. In each book, this funny, adventuresome series transports children back in time to one of America's 50 states.

The kids at Archie Beller's new school are the weirdest kids in America. Because in Kings Cove, California, kids don't do things like ride bikes, play video games, and read comic books. **Nope, in Kings Cove you're either a Pirate, or you're a Ninja.** And Archie... well, he just wants to be a normal kid from Nebraska. But when these weird kids force Archie to choose a side, **something goes horribly wrong.** Will Archie find his way out of trouble so he can lead the life of a normal kid? Or will he be forced into leading a double life? By day, a normal quiet kid. By night, America's newest crime fighter, a brave superhero known to friend and foe as... PIRATE NINJA!!!

For ten year-old Remi Muldoon, being SMALL is a BIG problem--especially with the kids at school.

And when Remi's attempt to become popular upsets the balance of the universe, things get worse. MUCH worse. Now, Remi must race against the clock to fix history before it's too late and along the way, he might just learn that the smallest of kids can have the biggest of lives.

Brought to life by Author/Illustrator Daniel Kenney, this hilarious first book in the Big Life graphic novel series is perfect for children ages 7-10.

Six months after his mom's death, a still broken-hearted Curial Diggs discovers that she has left him a challenge.

His mom wants him to find The Romanov Dolls, a fantastic treasure stolen from the Manhattan Art Collective when she was only a child. Despite having an overbearing famous father - who has already mapped out his son's future - Curial follows his heart and his mother's clues to Russia where he teams up with the granddaughter of a Russian History Professor to unravel the mystery behind the priceless treasure. Full of history, humor, and danger, Teenage Treasure Hunter is perfect for readers ages 10-14.

ABOUT THE AUTHORS

DANIEL KENNEY

Daniel Kenney is the children's author behind such popular series as *Project Gemini*, *The Big Life of Remi Muldoon*, *The History Mystery Kids*, *The Science Inspectors*, and *The Math Inspectors*. He and his wife live in Omaha, Nebraska, where they enjoy screaming children, little sleep, and dragons. Because who doesn't love dragons? To learn more go to www.DanielKenney.com.

EMILY BOEVER

Emily Boever was born with an overactive imagination. She spent much of her childhood convinced she was The Incredible Hulk and adventuring with three imaginary friends. When she grew too old to play with friends no one else could see, she turned her imagination to more mature things like studying, traveling, and teaching. Only after marrying her wonderful husband, Matt, and having kids of her own did Emily discover that she was finally old enough to reunite with her imaginary friends (and even add a few new ones) in the pages of her own books. Emily and Matt live with their kids in Omaha, Nebraska. Find more information at www.EmilyBoever.com.

CPSIA information can be obtained
at www.ICGtesting.com
Printed in the USA
LVHW04s1618200418
574264LV00002B/421/P